Letters To The Little Flower - The Gift of Spiritual Companionship With St. Therese of Lisieux

Peggy Phillips

Published by Pradera Rosa Publishing House, 2022.

This is a work of fiction. Similarities to real people, places, or events are entirely coincidental.

LETTERS TO THE LITTLE FLOWER - THE GIFT OF SPIRITUAL COMPANIONSHIP WITH ST. THERESE OF LISIEUX

First edition. November 20, 2022.

Copyright © 2022 Peggy Phillips.

ISBN: 979-8201323790

Written by Peggy Phillips.

Table of Contents

To my mother, my first sage along the journey of my Catholic faith formation, and my father, my lifelong sage whose steadfast encouragement revealed my joy in the creative expression of writing.

Introduction

Marvel at the petals of Divine Providence that mark every turn of the journey.

Empty nester Marise Gallica uncovers a peculiar envelope in a shuttered elementary school, which inspires her to write a collection of narratives about her life through letters to St. Thérèse of Lisieux, The Little Flower.

Seeking informal guidance, she emails her narratives to her former high school teacher, Mr. Theodore Locherbie, the legendary sage of Honors English at Victory Prep Academy, who delivers his keen remarks through his email responses.

But when she announces plans to publish her narratives, her siblings' withering rebuke paralyzes Marise with shame. Bereft in her tenuous family ties, Marise embarks on a tumultuous journey destined to reveal her original identity.

An epistolary novella that captures the experience of being human, Letters to The Little Flower celebrates the gift of spiritual companionship with St. Thérèse in the journey to discovering who God created you to be.

Chapter 1 The Teacher

From: Marise Gallica

To: Theodore Locherbie

Subject: Greetings from a former student

Hello Mr. Locherbie,

I am Marise Gallica. I was a student in your Honors English class decades ago at Victory Prep Academy. I'm contacting you because I'm seeking guidance on an epistolary novella I'm authoring, *"Letters to the Little Flower."*

I can think of no person better suited for the task than you, Mr. Locherbie, the legendary sage of Honors English at VPA. I am reaching out to you because you have the sensibility and keen insight to assess the suitability of my narratives for publication.

For example, do my stories elicit emotion? Might they motivate the reader to ponder her insecurities, identity, ego, and relationships? More so, do my narratives express the truth of the human experience?

Indeed, I would be honored if you, Mr. Locherbie, could offer insight into the literary quality of my book. I look forward to hearing from you soon.

Regards, Marise

To: Marise Gallica

From: Theodore Locherbie

Subject: Greetings from a former student

Marise,

It's great to discover that you still have a penchant for creative writing; I still remember that you showed a depth of insight and a creative, sensitive side when you were in high school. I will gladly provide insights into what you have written.

I could look over anything you send me during Christmas break, although I will be immersed in grading papers and working with students until then.

I could send you a copy of my upgraded punctuation and grammar rules, which should address any mechanics issues or questions you might have.

However, from your correspondence with me, I can see that you already have proficiency in these concepts.

I would be honored to evaluate your narratives.

Regards, Theodore Locherbie

To: Theodore Locherbie

From: Marise Gallica

Mr. Locherbie,

I'm thrilled you are eager to review my manuscript, and I am ready to forward my first narrative. Note, however, that my book is a work in progress, and I will send you chapters as I complete them.

But first, may I offer background about St. Thérèse of Lisieux and my connection to the saint, which you may find helpful, especially if you are not of the Roman Catholic faith.

St. Thérèse of Lisieux, who was a French nun and mystic, also is known as "St. Thérèse, The Little Flower" and "St. Thérèse of the Child Jesus." The Roman Catholic Church esteems St. Thérèse as a Doctor of the Church for her profound theology of divine love.

The saint dedicated her life to doing "ordinary things with extraordinary love," as she wrote in her autobiography, "performing small acts unknown to others, to give glory to God alone."

A prolific writer, she created her most significant work upon her deathbed at age twenty-four amidst the agony of tuberculosis. Indeed, her words, "I will let fall from heaven a shower of roses," portray the symbol by which The Little Flower shares her friendship with those who seek her intercession.

Catholics do not pray to saints. Instead, Catholics seek spiritual companionship with saints. For Catholics in English-speaking countries, this saint might be one's patron saint, a saint with whom they identify and thus chose as their Confirmation name for the Sacrament of Confirmation.

As a child, I chose St. Thérèse, The Little Flower, as my patron saint for Confirmation when I was ten. But I only learned of the saint on a wintry Saturday morning in February, two years before my Confirmation.

I was with my mother in the kitchen when my father dropped an armful of mail on the table. Two cartons of books tumbled to the floor. My horse books arrived!

In the 1970s, I was among the dwindling population of kids who yearned for a real horse. But my parents harbored no intention of indulging me.

Instead, my mother subscribed me to a book club, which each month delivered two classics of childhood equine literature. When my books arrived, I would tear open the carton with unbridled abandon and sequester myself from the chaos of the household to indulge in my new books.

That morning was no different. Except, I opened the other carton first. Inside was a text-dense book, "*The Story of Thérèse Martin,*" featuring a black and white photograph of a teenage girl on its cover.

My mother subscribed to a book club, too. But hers were inspirational books—not horse books.

"What's this book?" I asked my parents, who were standing nearby.

"It's a book about St. Thérèse," my mother smiled.

"Who's that?" I queried with the wide-eyed curiosity of an eight-year-old.

"She was a nun who became a saint known as 'The Little Flower,'" my mother said. Intrigued, I continued my press. "Why was she called that?"

She believed that you don't have to do big things to get to heaven or to be a saint, my mother explained.

St. Thérèse believed that the "little way" can get you to heaven—if you simply do the little things God needs you to do but do them all with love.

I peered at my father, who stood nearby with a twinkle in his eyes.

"You remind us of St. Thérèse," my mother remarked. "She was the youngest of a large family of girls and was very close to her father."

"Ok," I noted with disinterest. Then, with my fleeting interest in the saint thus satisfied, I trotted to a quiet corner of the house to read my new horse book.

Two years later, in preparation for Confirmation, I chose St. Thérèse of Lisieux for my patron saint, when as a ten-year-old, I pronounced her name as "St. 'Terése'" ([Teh-REES]), the English pronunciation.

Yet, I chose the saint not for her profound theology of love or her motto of "The Little Way." Instead, I chose St. Thérèse only in giddy anticipation of hearing our names rhyme when the bishop announced my Confirmation name: "Marise-Therese."

Only years later would I recognize the truth in the old Catholic adage, "we do not choose our patron saints; they choose us."

Indeed, for a girl who loved the beauty of words and language, who could be a more fitting patron saint than St. Thérèse, whose name rhymes with Marise, "Marise-Thérèse."

So, my novella, *"Letters to the Little Flower,"* recounts how I, decades later, discovered the gift of spiritual companionship with my long-forgotten patron saint, St. Thérèse of Lisieux, The Little Flower.

Regards, Marise

Chapter 2 The Classroom

To: Theodore Locherbie

From: Marise Gallica

Subject: "The Classroom"

Mr. Locherbie,

I'm thrilled that you've agreed to review my narratives. I've attached for your review my first story, "*The Classroom.*"

My narratives are based on the Catholic faith tradition and thus may resonate with Catholics of all ilk—cradle Catholics, lapsed Catholics, reverted Catholics, and converts.

I've composed a collection of "letters" to St. Thérèse, which I hope will be a cohesive narrative of my spiritual journey, and I'm seeking substantive feedback on my work.

Do my stories build tension and evoke emotion? Do they pique your curiosity to read further? Or do my stories read like sentimental drivel?

Thank you again, Mr. Locherbie, for agreeing to lend your editorial expertise to my project.

Regards, Marise

Dear St. Thérèse,

Today is my birthday, and I'm delighted to share that I received a most unexpected and curious birthday gift on a bookshelf in a classroom in the shuttered Catholic elementary school, Jesus Sun of Justice Academy.

The Classroom

I spent my birthday this year serving my parish at Jesus Sun of Justice Church, which marked the church's last occupancy date in its sixty-year-old building.

Parish volunteers were dismantling the sixty-year-old building and its adjacent grade school that day in preparation for the building's demolition, which would make way for our new church and school. So, I volunteered to photograph the day's activity.

I stepped from the worship area where the volunteers were removing pews and headed toward the dilapidated wing that once housed the school's classrooms.

I'd heard of the run-down school and wanted to see the old classrooms before construction crews demolished them.

I halted at the entrance of the school's hallway and peered into the darkness, illuminated only by the gray crescent of light emanating from the first room on the left.

The only room still safe for use, the former seventh-grade classroom, was used for choir practice after the school relocated ten years ago to a temporary building two miles away.

Indeed, earlier that morning, someone propped open the classroom door in anticipation of the movers, who would haul the piano to a temporary home while the new church and school were under construction.

Upon stepping into the classroom, I stood unmoving for a moment to absorb the presence of the space—the drab, windowless walls, threadbare carpet, and dusty bookshelves heavy with mathematics, literature, and geography textbooks.

I could only imagine the countless students, teachers, and lessons the room saw during its forty-year tenure as a classroom.

Intrigued by the textbooks lining the bookshelves, I pulled a random, blue-spine geography text from a nearby low shelf and flipped open its battered front cover, noting the book's 1975 copyright.

How sad, I sighed. The old school saw its last class in 2008, yet its meager resources could provide only sorely outdated textbooks for its students, primarily Black students who lived in poverty.

I leaned over to return the textbook to its original station on the bookshelf, where I glimpsed a book with an image of a white rose on its cover wedged behind the geography textbooks.

Unable to contain my curiosity, I yanked the geography textbooks from the shelf and then extracted the wayward book, *The Photo Album of St. Thérèse of Lisieux*, its ragged book jacket graced with a sketch of the white rose.

The photo album was published in 1962 and featured forty-seven photographs of the saint's childhood and nine years as a nun at the Convent of Carmel in Lisieux, France. According to the foreword, the album represents the last significant historical material released by Carmel to the public.

But no less intriguing was the envelope I discovered inside the aging photo album. The envelope, marked "Letters to The Little Flower," contained neither letters to the saint nor anyone but only a crease-worn, accordion-folded Kansas road map.

Yet, the envelope's odd contents suggested neither the meaning of its title nor why it resided inside the photo album on a bookshelf in the shuttered classroom.

But the peculiar envelope nonetheless inspires me to document the narratives of my own life in a collection of my own "letters" to St. Thérèse of Lisieux, The Little Flower.

To: Marise Gallica
    From: Theodore Locherbie

Subject: Response to your book idea

Marise, What an original idea! I'm eager to read your subsequent "Letters" to your patron saint.

Regards, Theodore Locherbie

Chapter 3 The Highway

To: Theodore Locherbie

From: Marise Gallica

Subject: "The Highway"

Mr. Locherbie,

Attached is my second letter to The Little Flower, a narrative that I can only describe as a numinous experience one night on a dark, dangerous highway years ago.

Regards, Marise

Dear St. Thérèse,

For weeks I've pondered the meaning of the Kansas road map inside the envelope labeled "Letters to The Little Flower." But I sense no connection between the map and the curious envelope.

Nonetheless, the map hearkens to my memory of a dangerous night on a dark highway five years ago, where I experienced the undeniable presence of God at the scene of a horrific accident.

I shared my story of that harrowing night two years later through a letter to Fr. Pepe, pastor of Jesus Sun of Justice Catholic Church, in my narrative, "The Highway."

In friendship, Marise

The Highway

Dear Fr. Pepe,

I'm writing to you, Father Pepe, to apologize for my recent unfavorable comments about the Catholic Church.

Indeed, your look of resignation upon hearing my comments spoke volumes about the demoralizing toll such words take on you as a pastor and person. For that, I am genuinely sorry for such demoralizing jabs. Please accept my apology.

Although I made pointed comments about the Church, I wish to explain why I feel the way I do. Unfortunately, the snippets of time when our paths cross after Mass afford a limited opportunity for meaningful dialog.

Hence, I blurt out what I'm feeling, believing I can deftly offer deeper context with softer edges on the fly while the rest of the congregation clamors for your attention behind me.

But logic and linguistic acumen escape me, so I clam up and move on. Nonetheless, I would like to share what I've shared in person through a letter.

My return to the Church began three years ago when my long-term significant other, Carl, and I decided to marry.

I contacted our family's long-time priest friend, Fr. Weston, about blessing the marriage. He informed me that I would need to attend Mass regularly, register in a parish, and then request that the parish priest bless the union.

So, as a disaffected Catholic for thirty years, I begrudgingly decided to make the token appearance of returning to the Church.

So, weeks later, I dropped into Saturday evening Mass at St. Augustine's, the home of my childhood Catholic faith formation.

I arrived twenty minutes before Mass to find a packed parking lot crammed with high-end automobiles.

Drivers barged through the driveway, defying basic traffic rules, while clusters of pedestrian churchgoers waited for a safe break to cross the parking lot. No one on the sidewalk smiled or made eye contact with me.

No one greeted me at the door. The pews were filling up, and no one moved over to make room for a party of one. Then, finally, an older man budged, and I squeezed in.

Lines at the confessionals were four deep, where I observed youth and adults texting on their smartphones while awaiting their turn in the confessional.

I sat back in the pew to meditate but was distracted by what I saw—and didn't see—filling the pews around me. I spied designer clothing and pricey youth sports club gear. But I saw no person different from me, a white, middle-class suburbanite.

The Catholic Church's "mystical body," as embodied by those I observed that night, was unchanged from when I drifted from the faith thirty years before: a fashion show for the privileged, white, and affluent who are blissfully unconcerned with social justice beyond the politically convenient issue of abortion.

Mass was about to start. I bolted for the door.

I sat in my car and prayed for the intercession of St. Jude, a patron saint of impossible situations, to help me find a church home that fit my values and needs.

So, too, I thanked God for abundant blessings, then left to spend the evening with my fiancé Carl and our twin sons, Gavin and Devin.

Two weeks later, wedding plans were ramping up, and I needed to iron out the church situation so that we could set a date.

So, I decided to visit Jesus Sun of Justice Church. It was in Carl's neighborhood and the only African American parish in the diocese.

That weekend, I attended the 11 a.m. Mass at Jesus Sun of Justice. The elements of the church community, which were palpably askew at St. Augustine's, fell into divine alignment that day.

Unlike at St. Augustine's, the ushers welcomed me. And when the choir sang the entrance hymn, my eyes welled with tears.

Finally! I found a church I could call my home. I prayed for guidance, a blessed marriage, and my children's well-being. I asked God to transform me.

God listened.

Two days later, while returning from a road trip with Carl and my two granddaughters, an uncanny string of coincidences put me at the scene of a horrific accident on the highway.

That night, I was roaring down the turnpike at seventy-five miles per hour when blinking red hazard taillights suddenly appeared in the darkness.

"Oh my God! A car stalled in my lane," I cried.

I tapped the brakes and tried to ease into the other lane, but traffic sped around me, preventing me from going around.

As I coasted to a crawl, I spotted a man standing on the shoulder between the concrete median and the road, waving his arms and shouting into the night air.

I pulled near the shoulder so as not to collide with the man and rolled down my window.

"Call nine-one-one!" he shouted. "I hit a woman."

"What?" I exclaimed, dumbfounded. "Where is she?"

"Over there!" he yelled, pointing over the concrete median toward the oncoming traffic.

I jumped from the car and scanned the eastbound lanes.

The stark headlights of oncoming traffic revealed the limp corpse of a young woman lying in the roadway. Yet, traffic in both directions neither slowed nor stopped.

"I killed a woman," the distraught man wailed, his words laced with indescribable anguish.

I took hold of his arm, clasping his hand in mine. "It's going to be ok," I reassured him. "I'm a nurse. You're going to be ok. What is your name?"

He uttered his name and then wailed, "I didn't see her. I didn't mean to hit her." Devastated, the man sank to the shoulder of the road in despair and buried his head in his hands.

I learned later from the accident report that the woman's car became disabled in the driving lane. She was standing outside her car when the vehicle driven by this man performed an evasive maneuver and struck her. The impact threw her body over the median into the oncoming traffic.

Suddenly, my heart pounded. My parked car was straddling the shoulder and the lane behind the stalled vehicle, placing us in grave danger of certain death from a high-speed rear-end collision.

My rational brain urged me to return to my car and leave the scene at once. But my heart begged me to stay with the man.

So, I peered into the darkness only to see the man walking away on the shoulder as if to remove himself from the scene.

Oh dear, I gasped; he might be in a state of dissociation—a condition in which a person is so upset they don't think clearly.

But, heeding my nursing instinct, I stayed calm and stayed with the young man lest he wandered into the oncoming traffic.

"Come over here," I called. "I will stay with you." I opened my arms and encircled the young man in a hug as backdrafts from the high-speed traffic swept past us.

He sank into my arms.

For a moment, the human connection forged when the despair of tragedy met a stranger's compassion transcended time, distance, and space.

In that instant, I was awash in peace, love, mercy, and goodness, as if there were no traffic, danger, and fear. This devastated young man and I and my beloved family were safe, enveloped by a warm, divine light.

Within minutes, the flashing lights of emergency vehicles appeared, and the man walked toward the emergency responders. I knew he was safe and that leaving was ok.

We pulled away and resumed our long trip home, during which my mind reeled with the anxiety of a near-miss trauma for myself and my family.

I pondered why an uncanny sequence of events put me on that highway that night.

My older son and his wife, who live three hours north, had planned an out-of-town vacation that week. But three days prior, their sitter backed out.

Desperate, they begged me, Grandma, to keep their two toddler-age girls. So I requested time off from my nursing job to care for my granddaughters the following day. Yet, despite the short notice, my employer granted my request, which is unusual in the nursing field.

Moreover, although I originally planned to stay overnight at my son's home and return with my grandchildren the next day, Carl offered to join me for the ride, so we arranged to return home that night.

Indeed, Carl and I spent a delightful evening with my son, daughter-in-law, and grandchildren, staying hours past our intended departure time.

So, as we bundled my grandbabies for the three-hour return trip home, my son recommended we take a different route to get us home faster. It was a route I wouldn't have taken, but it was where I encountered the accident.

Unable to sleep, I pondered how we emerged unscathed from such a perilous situation. Finally, I got up to fold laundry, where I spied my bright red Kansas City Chiefs t-shirt, which I'd worn the night of the accident. I noted the striking gold and white arrowhead logo on the front.

Minutes before leaving for the trip, inexplicably, I changed out of a dark blue t-shirt into the Chiefs t-shirt. Did the bold red t-shirt with a gold decal catch the eyes of oncoming motorists, allowing them time to switch lanes? I could only wonder.

I replayed the accident scene and recalled the image of a front-end grill and headlamps from a tractor-trailer, which pulled to a stop behind our car.

I could only recall how the truck provided much-needed light and a safety buffer for five vulnerable persons at the scene of an accident on the dark, high-speed highway.

I grappled with the guilt that I should've done things differently to not endanger my loved ones. Yet, as a human being, a nurse, a mother, and a citizen, I did the right thing.

The experience rekindled my pride in my nursing training. It called forth deep maternal instincts to protect a vulnerable human being. It summoned courage I never knew I had.

But, most profoundly, the coincidences that put me in that time and space that night awakened a slumbering spiritual consciousness to the goodness, mercy, and wisdom of a higher power.

So, Fr. Pepe, this is the story of my road back to the Church. Indeed, I get angry that conservative Catholics commandeer the Church for political gain.

But, as my sister, Miriam, who is a religious sister with the Congregation of Merciful Jesus (CMJ), reminds me, "It's my Church, too!"

You are an inspiring pastor, and I thank God for the blessing of your preaching.

Respectfully, Marise Gallica

To: Marise Gallica

    From: Theodore Locherbie

    Subject: Remarks—"The Highway"

    Marise,

I've finished reading "The Highway." I especially appreciated your critique of today's social elitism and spiritual blindness in churches. As such, the beginning of your spiritual journey may resonate with current or former church attendees of any denomination.

I hoped the story might show a stronger connection between the accident experience and your spiritual awakening and "sojourn back to Church."

Did you feel a divine nudge after this experience to draw closer to God by becoming part of a corporate worship experience or church and hearing His Word more consistently and deeply from a respected parish priest?

Otherwise, I'd like to know if your past experiences with your faith tradition lacked spiritual depth. Still, your encounter with a "God presence" at the accident scene and the various coincidences, which might be "God-incidences," have captivated your spirituality and moved you to seek greater spiritual depth within your faith tradition.

Marise, this Highway story provides a worthy foundation for the genesis of a spiritual awakening journey. I'm eagerly waiting to read your second entry.

Regards, Theodore Locherbie

To: Theodore Locherbie

 From: Marise Gallica

 Subject: "Laetare Sunday"

 Mr. Locherbie,

 I wouldn't call my numinous experience on the highway a modern-day version of St. Paul the Apostle's Road to Damascus experience of conversion.

 In fact, I had no intention of reverting to my Catholic faith; I was only looking for a priest to officiate my wedding.

Indeed, the synchronicity around the accident –the simultaneous occurrence of events that appear significantly related but have no discernible causal connection–might've been a "divine nudge" to spiritual awakening.

But ironically, God invited my spiritual transformation, not through synchronicity around that perilous night, but through the movement of the Holy Spirit two years later, after I shared my highway story narrative with Fr. Pepe.

Regards, Marise

Chapter 4 Laetare Sunday

Dear St. Thérèse,

My journal story, "Laetare Sunday," describes the circumstance that moved me to share my narrative, "The Highway," and the unanticipated aftermath of my sharing it.

In friendship, Marise

Laetare Sunday

The fourth Sunday of Lent, Laetare Sunday, held special significance for me this year.

As the congregation sang songs of joy in observance of Laetare Sunday, my heart sang songs of joy in my renewed trust in God. Two days earlier, the inner disquiet that consumed me for months ended.

These past few months, I have missed Mass for two weeks. Those two weeks led me to spiritual desolation over four ongoing trials since last fall. The disquiet began last fall when I sent a letter to Fr. Pepe, pastor of Jesus Sun of Justice Church.

The Saga

The saga of my letter began on a warm, windy Sunday, the last weekend of September. Disgruntled at Fr. Pepe's announcement of a local pro-life rally, I registered my dissatisfaction as I passed the priest after Mass.

In fact, so angry was I at the anti-abortion fervor of the Catholic Church to the exclusion of other life issues that I resolved that day to sever all association with the Church.

"I'm not in favor of abortion," I remarked over the phone to my older son, Julian. "But while the Church fervently protests abortion, too many Catholics stay conspicuously silent to the tragic social disparities that so often compel a mother to make the tragic choice of abortion."

Hence, in protest of the Church's anti-abortion fervor, I did not attend Mass for the next four weeks.

But with each passing Sunday, I sensed an emptiness of spirit, which I could only attribute to missing Holy Communion. I needed to go back—Church and politics notwithstanding.

Likewise, although Fr. Pepe had moved on from my discontented commentary about his sermon, I wanted to make amends, nonetheless.

I dropped into Mass on a Tuesday evening after work, intending to convey no hard feelings toward the priest by my presence. But I never expected that upon receiving Holy Communion that night, my soul would descend into a crucible of angst from which it would not emerge for months.

As I waited with hands cupped to receive the host in my palm, Fr. Pepe touched my hand in goodwill, a kind gesture intended to welcome me back and signal no hard feelings. Intuitively, I knew this. But I flinched!

Numb with embarrassment, I nodded silently when I passed by the priest after Mass and then trod a hasty exit for the door. I could only speculate what Fr. Pepe suspected would cause me to flinch—dislike, distrust, anger, or fear.

I needed an amicable and meaningful way to communicate to Fr. Pepe that none of those applied. No doubt, I had the ideal means: my compelling story of experiencing God's presence at the scene of a highway accident and its precursor, the story of my return to the Church.

My highway story is spiritually significant and personally meaningful but not excruciatingly personal.

So, I journaled *"The Highway"* and shared it with select friends and family, who received it favorably. I couldn't think of a more fitting personal story to share with a priest.

Moreover, my then-fiancé Carl and I planned to share the highway story over dinner with Fr. Pepe after our prenuptial counseling two years ago. But the dinner plans never transpired.

So now, sharing the story with Fr. Pepe would be a benign self-disclosure. More so, given that self-disclosure calls for a degree of trust, I presumed that Fr. Pepe would receive it favorably; trust would be implicit in my sharing the story.

The following week, I attended Tuesday evening Mass, the second anniversary of my return to the Church. I planned to catch Father Pepe after Mass and verbalize an abridged version of my return-to-Church and highway stories.

But alas! My well-planned exchange unfurled as follows:

"Hello, Fr. Pepe. Today is the second anniversary of my return to the Church," I said enthusiastically.

"How did you return to the Church?" he replied flatly.

"I went to Mass at St. Augustine's, which was awful!" I responded emphatically.

He returned a blank gaze, suggesting a weariness of hearing malcontent comments over his forty years as a priest.

"There's more to it...." I stammered as I slipped out the door.

With the exchange run aground, I concluded there never would be an apt time to tell Fr. Pepe the highway story.

Moreover, verbalizing the story wouldn't do justice to the emotional nature of the experience, as would my journal narrative.

"That's it!" I exclaimed to myself. "I'll share my story with Fr. Pepe through a letter!"

That night I composed a letter to Fr. Pepe, which described my return to the Church and then segued into the more meaningful purpose of my message: The story of my numinous experience on the highway.

I mailed my letter the next day. I presumed that once Fr. Pepe read it, he would mention "what an amazing story" the next time I passed him after Mass, and thereby I could resume my status as merely a parishioner at his church.

I never suspected my letter to the priest would create a merciless roil of self-disclosure angst.

Of course, when self-disclosure is received favorably, the relationship stays at a minimum on favorable terms. But when self-disclosure goes unfavorably, the ensuing anguish endured by the one who disclosed is akin to a vial of toxin, afflicting the relationship with shame.

So how might self-disclosure unfold? Let me count the ways.

The Uncertainty

My letter about the highway accident uncapped the vial of uncertainty angst.

For months after receiving my letter, Fr. Pepe acknowledged me with an ardent handshake as I departed Mass each Sunday.

He routinely verbalized genuine intentions to respond to my "sweet letter," at which I mumbled, "No worries," with my head down and eyes averted in a self-conscious posture.

Nonetheless, I was at a loss to ascertain how the priest received my disclosure of experiencing God's presence at the scene of a highway accident.

In his forty years as a diocesan priest, Fr. Pepe no doubt encountered parishioners of all ilk.

Did the priest believe my story, or did he receive it with jaded skepticism? Did he perceive me as a needy, bored, or lonely parishioner with nothing better to do than write letters to the priest?

Worse, did my letter serve to typecast me as the cringe-worthy female seeking attention from the pastor.

The Avoidance

Unable to tether my angst, I sought a second opinion from an older nurse friend, Connie, who lived five hundred miles away. I felt safe with Connie and trusted she would offer sage insight into my situation.

So, I emailed her, describing the circumstance and disclosing my angst over my letter to the priest. But she never responded.

Connie's awkward silence uncorked the vial of avoidance angst, which ensues when disclosure goes unacknowledged.

I anxiously checked my email for Connie's response for weeks, only to be crestfallen when none appeared. Her interminable silence overwhelmed me, for I had never felt so exposed yet invisible.

The Invalidation

More so, my letter to the priest led to the anguish of being invalidated by Carl, my spouse.

As I mailed the letter, I recalled my offer to donate my burial plot to Jesus Sun of Justice Church. While arranging the donation with the cemetery office that day, I purchased a memorial brick for my sibling, David, who died as a pre-term infant when I was a baby.

Years ago, I mentioned the story of David's death to Carl, but I rarely spoke of David in the intervening years.

Yet when I disclosed my brick purchase to Carl, he invalidated my reason for it, at which the shame of being invalidated by my spouse compounded the tumult of my self-disclosure anguish.

The Suppression

My anxiety over self-disclosure to the priest, my friend, and my spouse exacted a toll on my job. This led to another layer of self-disclosure anxiety, which ensues when the circumstance disallows disclosure.

Eight months prior, I'd resigned from a lucrative job as a nurse at a smaller hospital for a similar position at a larger hospital, which offered the prospect of career advancement.

But I soon discovered the new job to be nothing as I expected.

Instead, from bureaucratic oversight and broken processes to greedy culture and passive-aggressive coworkers, my workdays were fraught with frustration, defeat, and disengagement.

Then, six months later, a blustery winter morning found me in the manager's office, reviewing my dreaded "Performance Improvement Plan," the corporate death knell for the underperforming employee.

"Marise," my manager said, "I sense resistance from you in embracing our culture."

I held my breath and girded for job termination, as my performance had yet to meet my employer's expectations. Albeit the cresting waves of disclosure angst throughout my workday weren't helping, I mused to myself.

"I'm putting you on a performance improvement plan," my manager continued, "so we can address your 'growth opportunities.'"

Relieved I still had my job, I wrestled with the anguish of suppressed disclosure.

I longed to disclose that my values, temperament, and work style were ill-suited for the soul-crushing environment and that I should resign.

But I suppressed disclosure of my discontent and tried to appear absorbed in my "improvement plan."

The Adoration Chapel

As the weeks passed, my disclosure angst drained me. Then, finally, I awakened one Sunday with the motivation to go to Mass all but vanished.

The prospect of communal worship that day struck me as distracting and irritating; instead, I yearned for quiet time alone in the presence of Christ.

So later that morning, I sought the sacred silence of the Adoration Chapel at the local Cana Retreat Center.

In the Catholic faith tradition, an adoration chapel is a dedicated space in a church for personal prayer to Jesus, who is present in a consecrated Eucharistic host.

This host is the Blessed Sacrament, the Real Presence of Jesus Christ, and praying in an adoration chapel is seen as sitting or kneeling in front of Jesus himself.

For the past few months, I took refuge from job stress at the Adoration Chapel, where my Adoration time became a comforting ritual to end my workday.

That Sunday, while meditating before the Eucharist, I petitioned God to resolve the exhausting disquiet in my soul.

"My disclosure angst and job stress exhaust me, God. I'm a nurse with a tenacious immune system and am rarely sick. Yet lingering pneumonia nearly consumed me throughout November, and in December, I lay ill in bed for three days with influenza.

"I can't sleep, and I've lost fifteen pounds without trying," I whispered.

"You know how I crave the kinesthetic joy of my daily run, God. Three months ago, I could throw dinner in the oven and return from a brisk five-mile run while it still cooked. But now, a leisurely run around the block depletes me to near collapse.

"And now, God, I've discovered that my marriage is hollow, and I'm one misstep away from losing my job," I whispered as heavy teardrops fell silently into the flowered silk scarf at my neck.

"Haven't you noticed God? I feel as if I'm invisible to you."

I needn't have despaired. God always notices.

The Symphony

Two days after my Sunday morning meditation at the Adoration Chapel, Carl called, asking if we were still on for an upcoming symphony concert.

I proposed the date night weeks before, as we hadn't spent time together for months. I envisioned us enjoying a special night at the symphony and reconnecting over gourmet coffee and my homemade apple pie.

But I delayed buying tickets because I doubted that we would go. In eighteen months since our marriage, our twenty-two-year relationship deteriorated from companionship to distance.

Carl's query about our date night delivered a breath of hope, but that hope expired before the call ended.

"What time will the concert get out?" Carl inquired over speakerphone.

"Probably around 10 p.m.," I replied. "Why do you ask?"

"There's a party at the club Saturday," he said. "All my friends and family will be there. So, I can still make it if the concert gets out by ten. You're welcome to join us."

I paused and then replied that I thought we would spend the evening reconnecting.

"I don't want to go straight home after the concert!" Carl replied emphatically. "Why would I want to go home when I could be out with my friends and family?"

His retort rendered me speechless, at which my angst over our marriage evaporated. Carl's idea of "date night" with me, his wife, spoke volumes about his low regard for the emotionally intimate commitment of marriage.

Carl is a good man, but he's not the partner I need. We could remain friends and amicable co-parents, but I would move on to go wherever God leads me.

That night marked the first time I considered ending my twenty-two-year relationship with Carl, despite our marriage two years ago.

The Journalist

The following day, I attended 11 a.m. Mass at Jesus Sun of Justice.

I don't recall Fr. Pepe's homily that day, but I remember my meditation after Holy Communion and its revelation.

Upon returning to my pew, I bowed my head and contemplated not the sacred mystery of the Holy Eucharist (as a good Catholic ought) but what would I mumble to Fr. Pepe when he greeted me after Mass.

"My angst over my letter to Fr. Pepe has grown wearisome," I prayed. "Can't you do something about this, God?"

No sooner did the closing hymn commence than God revealed the seed of my angst.

It's not my story per se, but my unclear motive for sharing it with the priest!

How could Fr. Pepe sense the link between my mortifying flinch at Holy Communion one week and my compelling need to disclose a personal story after Mass the following week?

A dialog about the flinch would be moot, I reasoned. But there was still time to apprise Fr. Pepe of my writing background, which thus might quell lingering uncertainty about my motive for sharing the story.

"Um... Fr. Pepe, I've been remiss," I mumbled to the priest after Mass.

He returned a puzzled look.

"I should've told you," I continued, "I used to be a journalist, and now I journal stories about my own life. So, for example, I journaled my highway story two years ago, and I thought you'd find it a compelling read."

"Your conversion is amazing," Fr. Pepe replied.

I cocked my head and furrowed my eyebrows quizzically.

"Your conversion since your encounter with the accident on the highway," he clarified. "I've watched you for two years, and your highway story is so personally meaningful."

I continued my pitch.

"I occasionally share my narratives with select friends and family. So, I can add you to my list if you'd like to read them. But I don't want to make you uncomfortable."

"Why would your stories make me uncomfortable?" Fr. Pepe queried.

I rolled my eyes askance and stammered, "Um... well... a parishioner writing letters to the pastor... that's a little out there, I'd think."

"That's how you express yourself," Fr. Pepe declared. "I would be honored to read your journal stories!" he pronounced, squaring his shoulders proudly beneath his green Sunday vestment.

Alas! That statement alone thus dispelled the staggering uncertainty over my letter to the priest.

The Votive Candle

With my disclosure angst over my letter and my marriage being resolved, the threat of losing my job consumed me.

Following my performance-improvement meeting with my manager, my workplace stress grew visceral.

Then, one Friday two weeks later marked my worst day since starting the position. I departed work that night, believing I would lose my job the following Monday.

I attended early Mass that Sunday. I slid into the pew next to the Langston family—Terrance, Tina, and their two college-age children, with whom I routinely shared the pew.

After Mass, I approached Tina and, summoning all the courage my introverted personality could muster, inquired if she might pray for me.

"What's going on?" she whispered with a gentle face.

I briefly disclosed my job situation.

"Let's light a candle and pray together," she suggested with kind enthusiasm.

We hooked elbows and made our way to the votive candles at the front of the sanctuary near the portrait of Jesus, The Divine Mercy.

We lit a white candle, and together we asked that God supplant me with strength and grace to do his bidding, be it at my current job or someplace else.

"Please, God, put me where you need me," I prayed before the flickering bank of candles as Tina bowed her head and squeezed my hand.

God noticed.

On a Friday afternoon two weeks later, I found myself at a table in the vacant chapel at the new Mercy Senior Care Hospital on the city's east side. Across from me sat the director of nursing.

Prepared for the gauntlet of a panel interview, I sat puzzled that no one else was there.

"We're going to skip the interview formalities," the director pronounced. "What do you need from me to bring you on board here?" she queried.

I sat speechlessly; I'd visited with her two days earlier for a brief phone interview, and now she was making me an offer?

I departed an hour later with an offer to be the nurse leader designated to establish a culture of compassionate care at the new hospital, where I would start my new post three weeks later.

The Fourth Sunday of Lent

Two days after my unanticipated job offer, I attended Mass at Jesus Sun of Justice on the Fourth Sunday of Lent. But as I settled into a pew, I gazed with interest at the rose-colored linens adorning the altar.

"Today is Laetare Sunday—a day to express hope and rejoice in anticipation of Easter," announced Fr. Pepe, who wore rose-colored vestments.

"The rose-colored altar linens and vestments represent joy in the promise of the paschal mystery," he explained.

"The Church recognizes Laetare Sunday as a temporary break from Lenten fasting and penance, a day of joy in preparation for the darkness of Christ's passion and death from Good Friday through Holy Saturday."

As Mass proceeded, I contemplated Laetare Sunday and its joy in the hope between darkness and light, death and resurrection, stagnation and transformation. Like Jesus on the cross, when I felt shamed and forsaken, I needed only to ask and thereby receive the Providential mercy of God.

God is good!

To: Marise Gallica

From: Theodore Locherbie

Subject: Comments—"Laetare Sunday"

Hello Marise,

The parallels you draw between "darkness" and "light" depict an intellectually agonizing period of profound despair.

Your creative metaphors for your season of darkness after self-disclosure and the ensuing enlightenment you found through the symbolism of hope on Laetare Sunday make this narrative especially moving.

The Symphony section is particularly telling of your relationship with your spouse. Indeed, it is ironic that while you hoped to enjoy the complex harmony of the symphony that night, you experienced the complex disharmony of your relationship instead.

How intriguing that our external world so often mirrors our subconscious!

This chapter might be difficult for readers, but that's why it might resonate with so many. Haven't we all experienced the vulnerability and anguish when self-disclosure meets with uncertainty, avoidance, or invalidation?

Equally distressing are when we yearn to self-disclose, but we suppress our disclosure because the circumstance does not allow it.

Regards, Theodore Locherbie

To: Theodore Locherbie

From: Marise Gallica

Subject: Remarks—"Laetare Sunday"

Mr. Locherbie,

I withheld putting words to paper for this story for weeks. To portray in granular detail the experience of my self-disclosure gone unfavorably would be to examine my vulnerability under the glaring spotlight of the most potent emotion—shame.

The prospect of such an undertaking rendered me emotionally numb for weeks and unable to compose my thoughts for writing.

Yet, to deflect the experience would neither let it live and make me whole nor let it die and let me move forward. But a reflection from the late Fr. Nouwen inspired me to journal my story.

Fr. Nouwen's reflection implies that writing can be a meaningful spiritual discipline; writing can help attune us to the stirring of our hearts and the depth of our emotions and thus give artistic expression to our experiences and memories.

More so, Fr. Nouwen suggests that through writing, we can claim what we have lived and thus integrate it more fully into our journeys. So, writing can become lifesaving for us and sometimes for others to read our work.

Indeed, this narrative captures the anguish of self-disclosure gone unfavorably, which may stir deep wounds of vulnerability for some readers.

Nonetheless, this story can serve to reassure others that the experience of feeling vulnerable is part of the experience of being human.

Regards, Marise

Chapter 5 David's Brick

To: Theodore Locherbie

From: Marise Gallica

Subject: "David's Brick"

Mr. Locherbie,

My next story, "David's Brick," speaks of the quiet work of the Holy Spirit—the breath of God that animates our relationships but whose presence we so often are unaware of.

Regards, Marise

Dear St. Thérèse,

I share my journal story, "David's Brick," which reflects the healing that can be ours through the fruit of the Holy Spirit.

Inspired by Fr. Pepe's encouraging words after Mass a few weeks ago, I composed "David's Brick."

I finished the story three weeks later in the predawn hush of a frost-laden Sunday morning.

Hours later, I attended early Mass where, ironically, Fr. Pepe's homily that day spoke of "the blessings that can be ours through the fruit of the Holy Spirit."

In friendship, Marise

David's Brick

The Letter and the Burial Crypt

Carl is a good man. He embraces fatherhood, and he loves our twin sons. He offers warm companionship, and we've shared years of happy memories.

Yet after a twenty-two-year relationship, the last two in marriage, I remain no more than the ideal girlfriend to him. I arrived at this insight only recently and only through the agency of a letter, a burial crypt, and a brick.

The letter I refer to recounts my compelling narrative of experiencing God's presence at the scene of an accident on a highway three years earlier.

The experience reframed my spiritual life from that of a disaffected Catholic to that of a reverted Catholic seeking a more profound understanding of my faith.

Then, two years after the accident, I shared my highway story with Fr. Pepe by way of that letter. So, thus began the story of "David's Brick."

As I mailed my letter that morning, I recalled my long-forgotten offer to donate my burial crypt at Assumption Cemetery to Jesus Sun of Justice Church for any parishioner who couldn't afford burial for a loved one.

I couldn't fathom what possessed me twenty years ago to purchase a burial crypt. I paused for a moment, bemused at how life changes a person.

Had my mother not purchased family plots in a nearby rural cemetery years ago, I would've urged my family to give me a green burial when I die.

The Baby David

I called the cemetery office that day to arrange the burial crypt donation. But while on hold for the secretary to gather the paperwork, I recalled the city's other Catholic cemetery, Calvary Cemetery.

"That's where David is buried," I exclaimed to myself.

My mind scrolled back to my childhood and young adulthood. When I was six months old, my mother had a miscarriage.

On December 21, 1964, she slipped and fell, causing a near-fatal hemorrhage and the loss of her unborn infant of eighteen weeks, whom she had named David.

My mother recounted how the priest-chaplain stopped at the door of her hospital room to inform her that he was taking the baby to Calvary Cemetery for burial, as was the practice.

He admonished her to "Stop feeling sorry for yourself and get past this. You have other children to care for."

Unlike pastoral care today, which embraces an understanding of loss and grief informed with compassion, such wasn't the norm in the 1960s.

In 1964, there was no holding of the deceased infant for the last time, no grief counseling, no support groups, and no memorials.

Instead, my mother grieved David's burial in an unmarked grave at Calvary. More so, she was painfully aggrieved that she could never confirm that David was baptized.

Obedient to the priest's admonishment, my mother returned home weeks later to resume the whole plate of duties as a full-time wife and homemaker with a large brood of children under the age of nine.

My father, a family doctor, turned his attention back to his demanding, small-town practice. More so, as well-meaning people are wont to do, friends and neighbors who swooped in to help the good doctor's family in my mother's absence all but disappeared upon her return from the hospital.

My mother, who processed her loss in isolation, slogged through the years in a fog of complicated grief that she could never resolve. As the years passed, she resisted suggestions for therapy or support groups.

Instead, my mother believed she was at fault for the miscarriage, and she held fast to her old-school Catholic formation that her long-suffering grief was the penance she must bear for her loss.

Over time, my mother put forth a valiant effort to put the loss of David behind her. But the rivulets of tears that streamed down her cheeks throughout the Advent season until she passed away at age seventy-eight spoke otherwise.

At those times, she would recount the traumatic story to us children:

She described her near-death experience during this life-threatening event, whereby she watched from above in what felt like spiritual form as the doctors worked feverishly to save her.

My father, a physician, stayed at her side and laid eyes on David, a perfectly knit little boy. She recounted a warm, divine light beckoned her, but she chose to return.

We always listened with sympathy but were at a loss for comforting words. Otherwise, any mention of our deceased sibling was taboo.

My mother's unresolved grief shaded her relationship with me.

As the youngest, I learned to blend in with the crowd of siblings. It was safer to be invisible. Through my worldview, my mother loved me as a good Catholic mother ought, but she didn't like me.

Finally, at age twenty-eight, with my relationship with my mother untenable and my self-esteem in tatters, I found a good therapist, and we started drilling down.

One day, I randomly mentioned David. The therapist paused and, in typical therapist fashion, remarked, "Tell me more."

She nodded her head pensively as I recounted the story of my mother's miscarriage.

By the end of the hour, we had a plan.

First, I would open a private conversation with my mother about David and suggest that my siblings and I purchase a grave marker.

Then, I would propose that we have a quiet memorial service with family at the graveside.

My naïve twenty-eight-year-old mind envisioned the grief evaporating with poignant tears, and my mother and I would reconcile and live happily ever after.

That proposal met with scourging outrage from my mother.

"No!" my mother hissed. "There will be no grave marker and no memorial for 'the baby'!"

Indeed, nearly thirty years after losing David, my mother still couldn't bear to say his name. So, how dare I tread on the sacred ground of my mother's grief!

That discussion marked my most grievous memory of my mother. That day, the notion of a memorial for David fled into hiding in the deep backwoods of my psyche.

Over the next twenty-five years, I rarely thought of David until that crisp autumn morning with the cemetery office on hold.

The Brick

The secretary returned to the line, and as we wrapped up the requisite paperwork, I casually inquired about purchasing a grave marker for David.

Unfortunately, the cemetery records for pre-term infants fifty years ago were incomplete.

Most pre-term infants were buried in a general plot, so I could not place a grave marker. But for one hundred twenty-five dollars, I could purchase a memorial brick with David's name and date of death.

Without pause, I bought a brick for David that day.

That night, I mentioned the brick to Carl, to whom I noted the story of David and the proposed memorial long ago but with scant details.

"I need to see if my sister can take me to the doctor next week," Carl responded, his stare glued to the TV.

Thinking I hadn't snagged his attention, I reissued my statement, to which he intoned,

"I said I need to see if my sister can take me to the doctor next week."

Given the edge in his voice, he had no intention of acknowledging my statement. Yet again, despite my wish to share something meaningful, he ignored me. So, I made no further mention of the brick for the next two months.

The cemetery office notified me two months later that my brick order was complete. I would find it inlaid in the brick walkway near the Pieta statue in the cemetery's southwest corner.

The secretary informed me that the walkway memorialized infants buried in unmarked graves at the cemetery. That night, I told Carl that I planned to visit the cemetery to see David's brick when the weather turned warmer.

"You need to let that go!" Carl huffed.

"Your mother did not want a grave marker for that baby when she was living, and you tried to disrespect her then. Now, you want to disrespect her wishes when she's dead?! I can see why your mother didn't like you!"

His response didn't surprise me. I learned long ago that invalidation was his preferred defense mechanism whenever I made myself emotionally vulnerable.

Nonetheless, I reasoned, Carl believes the brick signifies merely a stone artifact memorializing the brother I never had a chance to know and love.

Perhaps lost on him was that the brick signifies a new interpretation of my relationship with my mother.

I began to speak to thus enlighten him. But he cut me off and stormed out of the room, terminating the discussion.

So, on a Saturday in late January, during a welcome respite from the bitter cold, I planned to visit the cemetery the next day. I invited Carl to join me.

"Marise, I can't get behind this," he retorted.

"What you're doing is disrespectful to your mother in her death, and you are wrong to do this. I could go with you and tell you what you want to hear," he bellowed. "But I would be lying, and I am not a liar. So I don't want to hear about this again!"

The Epiphany

Ignore. Invalidate. Rebuff. I was familiar with Carl's defensiveness whenever I invited him into a more meaningful understanding of who I am.

Were his rebuffs in speaking about any other part of me, I would have deemed them inconsequential to our relationship.

But my relationship with my mother sculpted my view of myself and my place in the world. So, to rebuke me for my relationship with my mother was to reject who I am.

Carl wanted no part of this most profound part of me—the substance and the soul. Yet, without the soul, where is the sanctity? Without sanctity, where is God? Without God, what is the purpose? It was an epiphany of epic spiritual proportion.

Theologian Fr. Henri Nouwen offers this thought on patience: "A waiting person is a patient person. Patience means the willingness to stay where we are and live the situation fully, believing that something hidden there will manifest itself to us."

I imagine Fr. Nouwen would concur that I have lived my relationship with Carl to its fullest.

Indeed, David's brick and the epiphany it led revealed the uncomfortable truth about the absence of emotional intimacy in my relationship with Carl—a reality I denied for years.

The Fruit of the Holy Spirit

The next day I stood not in communal worship at Jesus Sun of Justice Church but in solitude on the brick walkway near the Pieta statue in Calvary Cemetery. At my feet lay David's Brick, "David Daniels December 21, 1964," upon which I placed a long-stemmed white rose.

I gazed at the brick and thought not of David but of my older son, Julian, now almost thirty years old.

Were it not for God's blessing of Julian, the relationship with my mother might have remained untenable. From age seven until he left for college, Julian was a daily presence in my mother's life.

Hence, over time, we reframed our relationship from one of discord to one of joy through our love of Julian.

Julian graduated high school as a decorated scholar, and after his graduation, I sat with my mother on a gloriously sunny day on the patio at my parents' home.

Together we reflected on Julian when the rare thought of David moved me to speak in our shared silence.

"Mom," I queried in a thoughtful voice, "Do you ever think of David?"

It was the first time I'd spoken of David since that grievous day years ago. She sat quietly and then turned to me, radiant with love.

"Yes, Marise, I think of David often," she replied thoughtfully, her eyes pooled with tears.

I recalled that moment vividly: As my mother spoke, she held my gaze and nodded as if withholding something she couldn't disclose, the nuance of a smile upon her lips.

I lingered near David's brick and contemplated my mother and the faith that sustained her. My mother, a devout Catholic, avowed the abundant grace that flowed throughout her life from her relationship with the Holy Spirit.

"No matter the hardship, offer it up to the Holy Spirit," she enjoined me throughout my life.

What did she know that she couldn't disclose that day? Then, the Holy Spirit revealed the truth.

We didn't need a memorial twenty-five years ago to repair our relationship. Instead, we needed the Holy Spirit and the fruit thereof: peace, joy, charity, patience, kindness, gentleness, generosity, goodness, faithfulness, and self-control.

Alas! My mother knew this! Through our love of Julian, the Holy Spirit restored our fragmented relationship.

I now understood why my mother couldn't disclose this truth on that glorious spring day. She knew that only in God's time would I realize that our relationship was restored through the Holy Spirit. Hence, the slight smile!

I gazed across the sunlit cemetery and imagined my mother there: I would wrap my arm around her frail shoulders and make our way along the walkway to David's brick.

We would place a white rose upon the brick, signifying that David, my mother, and myself are innocent, beloved children of God. And together, we would weep with joy at the blessing of the Holy Spirit.

God is Good!

To: Marise Gallica

From: Theodore Locherbie

Subject: "David's Brick" remarks

Marise,

This story reflects the powerful revelations that provided the needed, helpful restoration of your relationship with your mother and insightful revelation of God's goodness.

This healing is especially evident in that your mother knew those revelations and that you recognized them for yourself as well, although much later in your journey.

I found particularly moving your reflections on your lifelong, contentious relationship with your mother and its connection to her unbearable grief after the miscarriage of your pre-born sibling.

Indeed, this narrative of losing a child to miscarriage may resonate with mothers who grieve the loss of their pre-born baby.

More so, this story offers hope for healing through the work of the Holy Spirit. Indeed, this narrative may resonate with daughters who grieve the mother-daughter relationships they never had.

Regards, Mr. Locherbie

Chapter 6 A Shower of Roses

To: Theodore Locherbie

    From: Marise Gallica

    Subject: "A Shower of Roses"

    Mr. Locherbie,

    My newfound spiritual companionship with The Little Flower, whose autobiography emboldened me to write "Laetare Sunday," inspired me to compose my latest story, "A Shower of Roses."

    Regards, Marise

Dear St. Thérèse,

My story, "A Shower of Roses," describes those unexpected occasions whereby mindfulness of the present moment illuminates the presence of God.

So too, this narrative portrays the blessings of your spiritual companionship, revealed to me through my unfolding journey of spiritual enlightenment.

This journey began when I encountered an accident on the highway three years ago.

In friendship, Marise

A Shower of Roses

The segue into this chapter of my spiritual enlightening began days after reading *The Story of a Soul—The Autobiography of St. Thérèse de Lisieux.*

I wouldn't have thought to read the book were it not for my New Year's resolution to unsubscribe from headline news on social media and instead devote thirty minutes daily to spiritual reading.

A family friend recommended a reading list that included works by the late Dutch priest and theologian Fr. Henri Nouwen. Since spiritual genre books never interested me, I was unfamiliar with Nouwen's work.

But over the first months of the year, I read two Nouwen books on my tablet, and one day, I noticed *The Story of a Soul* as a suggested read.

I hadn't thought of the saint since childhood, when I chose St. Thérèse Lisieux, "The Little Flower," as my patron saint for Confirmation. In fact, I received a statue of the saint as a Confirmation gift from my mother.

Indeed, the plaster statue of the Carmelite nun in her gold habit, her arms laden with roses and a crucifix, graced my dresser for years while I was growing up. But the statue shattered in transit during a move in my young adulthood, and I never replaced it.

Now, forty-five years later, mere curiosity motivated me to read about the life and spirituality of the French nun and mystic. But by the time I finished her story, my soul thirsted for the blessing of spiritual companionship with The Little Flower.

The Calling Card

I sought the spiritual companionship of The Little Flower for the first time two weeks later, in mid-April, when I prayed my first novena to St. Thérèse, the Novena of 24 Glory Be's.

In the Catholic faith tradition, a novena is nine days of private or public prayer, seeking the intercession of a saint or holy figure to obtain special graces, implore special favors, or make special petitions. (Novena is derived from the Latin *novena* meaning nine.)

According to the 24 Glory Be novena origin, if the petitioner receives a white rose, then St. Thérèse has heard the petition.

So, beginning Monday, April 9, I petitioned St. Thérèse's intercession to the Holy Spirit for guidance on my relationship with Carl.

"Please help me know God's will for my relationship with Carl, my spouse," I prayed that week during my daily visits to the Adoration Chapel at the Cana Retreat Center.

"Our relationship is at an impasse, and I have no one to talk to who understands. "And with all due respect," I added, "I adore roses, but I need a friend, not a rose."

As I left for work five days later, I noticed with dismay the violas in the garden near my doorstep. Although an early spring bloomer, the fragile ground creeper showed no sign of buds.

For the past four years, the lone viola—the only seed to sprout from a dime-store seed packet—emerged from its garden bed every spring but never yielded more than one bedraggled bloom.

I should extract it the next time I weed and relieve it of its misery, I mumbled as I headed to work.

That day at work, Brenda, my supervisor at my new job for two weeks, invited me to an impromptu lunch. So, naturally, the conversation turned to children and marriage.

I shared with Brenda the problem of marriage to a good man and a caring father who cannot tolerate emotional intimacy.

"He tells me to get my head fixed, and then we can have a relationship because there's nothing wrong with him," I whispered across the table. "I feel defeated. Invalidated. Invisible."

Brenda studied me with compassion.

"Marise, it's not you," she consoled me. "So many men grow up believing that they cannot let themselves be vulnerable. So when their partner is emotionally vulnerable with them, they fear that responding with empathy or understanding makes them vulnerable."

"I know how you feel," she continued. "I've been married for decades, but my husband finally got it only six years ago.

"Only through spending time with a couple from our church did he learn that emotional intimacy is the glue of marriage. But I couldn't change him; it took another man to show him what it means."

We never had the chance to visit again. The hospital terminated Brenda the following week, and we lost touch. But she was the friend I needed that day, and her understanding, insight, and kind words stayed with me.

As I made my way up my front walk that afternoon, a snippet of color in the garden near my doorstep caught my eye.

To my astonishment, the forlorn viola wore a tiara of flowers atop its leaves—small, spring-fresh blooms, cradled in a winter's nest of leaves starched crisp and brown by the chill of autumn's breath.

A colorful genus of the violet family, the violas called to mind a famous spiritual pearl penned by St. Thérèse' in her autobiography.

"In Jesus' Garden of souls, these must be content to be daisies or violets destined to give joy to God's glances when he looks down at His feet."

The rational nurse in me believed the physics of nature forced the flowers to bloom after four years of dormancy. But the hopeful believer in me saw the signature of St. Thérèse in the flowers at my feet.

I smiled and bowed my head in reverence to the humble saint. I needed a friend, and, with perfect timing, St. Thérèse delivered the friend I needed. I needed not a rose but simply to know my saint heard my prayers.

Thus, the Doctor of the Church left her calling card for me instead, a clutch of cheerful blooms in gold and violet and lavender hues bobbing in the playful breeze of a springtime afternoon.

My soul embraced the violas in unexpected bloom as an invitation to befriend my patron saint, petition The Little Flower's help, and share in the treasure of spiritual kinship with the Saint of the Child Jesus.

My perceived invitation to her spiritual friendship was timely indeed, for as the warm skies of spring yielded to the scorching heat of summer, great would be my thirst for the spiritual companionship of St. Thérèse.

The Tabernacle

I made a second novena to St. Thérèse two weeks later, petitioning her intercession for guidance on my next story, "Laetare Sunday." A profoundly personal narrative that portrays the vulnerability of self-disclosure gone unfavorably, this story was challenging to write.

Nonetheless, a meditation by the late Fr. Henri Nouwen inspired me to compose "Laetare Sunday." The reflection by the Dutch priest and author suggests that sharing our stories through writing can be good and even lifesaving for others.

Despite my motivation to write the narrative, I could find neither the clarity nor the words to express the tormenting but oh-so-very human experience of vulnerability when self-disclosure goes unfavorably.

And so, for eight days, I sought my patron saint's intercession through my daily prayer in the Adoration Chapel.

First, I placed a folded copy of my latest draft near the tabernacle, which sits atop a majestic boulder in the center of the Chapel. Then, I prayed the 24 Glory Be's for the saint's intercession to overcome my shame.

On the ninth day, despairing at my fruitless effort, I placed my draft near the tabernacle again, prayed the Glory Be's, and then sat back in a chapel chair.

"I can't write this," my discouraged soul conceded silently to St. Thérèse. "It's too complicated. I want to let it die."

Finally, with resignation, I gazed at the bronze tabernacle atop the boulder, awash in the pink light of a spring sunset pouring through the chapel windows.

Then, I closed my eyes and surrendered.

Instead of praying and asking, needing, and seeking, I contemplated St. Thérèse and the prolific expression of writing she created in her short life.

A gifted writer, she composed on paper that which was in her heart. With untold conviction, the saint believed her writing was a worthy expression of her soul, at which God smiled when he glanced down at The Little Flower.

I directed my eyes to the tabernacle bathed in the mellow light of the sinking sun. Yet, as I peered at the bronze sanctum safeguarding the Holy Eucharist, my soul intuited what my patron saint might intimate to me if she were with me there:

"Marise, my friend, deflecting your story will neither let it live and make you whole nor let it die and let you move forward.

"Believe with conviction that what you compose is a worthy expression of your soul, if only to give joy to God when he glances down at your work."

The words of encouragement that I intuited from my patron saint lifted the weight of unworthiness I attached to my story.

So, that night, I set forth with renewed confidence to compose "Laetare Sunday," a narrative I believed was destined only for the glance of God as a humble violet at his feet. Or so I thought.

The Nod

I made appreciable progress on the story over the following week, thoughts once murky sharpened with clarity and prose once bland and clumsy rebirthed with expression and grace.

Yet, as the story took shape, I wondered if I should share it with those in my trusted circle.

In mid-May, I initiated my third Glory Be novena, requesting The Little Flower's intercession for guidance on whether to share my story. A profoundly personal narrative, "Laetare Sunday" was my most challenging writing work.

"Please offer me a sign as to whether I should share this story," I prayed silently within the sacred space of the Adoration Chapel.

"And I'm sure you understand, St. Thérèse," I added, "that I needn't receive a rose as a sign you've heard my prayer."

I was astute enough to realize that a "rose" could signify grace and that my saint heard the prayer.

Indeed, had I not recently observed a host of nuanced graces from God: the friend at lunch, the violas in unexpected bloom, and the encouragement at the tabernacle?

So, I would watch for subtle signs that St. Thérèse heard my prayer, but not for a rose. Besides, I had no reason to expect a rose from anyone.

I attended early Mass at Jesus Sun of Justice Church the following Sunday, Mother's Day, and the fifth day of my novena. At the close of Mass, Fr. Pepe announced that the Knights of St. Peter Claver would be in the vestibule after Mass to give a Mother's Day rose to any mother who wanted one.

My heart lurched! A rose? Since joining Jesus Sun of Justice parish, I couldn't recall the Knights giving roses on Mother's Day. But, had I received one, I would've remembered.

While I've received mixed floral arrangements over the years, the only rose I'd ever received was at my high school graduation ceremony, where graduates received a long-stemmed white rose with their diplomas.

Over the next thirty-six years, I never received a rose for any occasion, neither from family, dating partners, platonic friends, or random persons.

Even Carl, in our twenty-two-year relationship, never indulged me with fresh flowers, which he decried as a waste of money.

After Mass, I navigated through the crowded entrance. An older gentleman wearing a Knight of St. Peter Claver fez offered me a long-stemmed white rose.

The rational nurse in me believed the rose to be a mere coincidence, a sign of synchronicity at best. But my soul beheld the rose as a flower from the heavenly garden handpicked by St. Thérèse as a message of love, especially for me.

But, alas, after nary a rose thirty-six years, how incredulous that I received, within the sacred space of Jesus Sun of Justice Church, a white rose while praying the Glory Be Novena to The Little Flower!

I prayed the remainder of the novena over the next four days in the peaceful presence of the Holy Eucharist in the Adoration Chapel, whereby my soul discerned the white rose to be a nod of confidence from the Doctor of the Church to share my story.

I would share it with the same conviction by which I authored it: The belief that my writing is a worthy expression of my soul and that those in my closest circle would see it as such.

For the next two weeks, I devoted a substantial fund of energy to the story. Finally, on Friday afternoon before Memorial Day, I finished the story.

I mailed the story to six select friends and family that day and then sat and exhaled with relief. Finally, after months of anxiety, I was eager to return to my old self. So, that weekend, I mapped out ambitious plans to revive the personal endeavors I abandoned a year ago in the fog of that disquiet.

Beyond the revival of those personal endeavors, of most significant import were the priceless moments I would spend with my teenage twin sons, Devin and Gavin.

My fifteen-year-old twins were heading into their sophomore year in high school, and this summer would be one of the few remaining where I could enjoy their daily presence in my home before they launched college. I yearned for the gift of presence in every precious moment with them.

The Friendship

The commencement of summer break promised a fresh start. I looked forward to spending time with Devin and Gavin, with whom I enjoyed a unique mother-son bond with each until two years ago. That was the impetus for my next novena to St. Thérèse.

Inherently affectionate, sensitive, and good-natured, Devin, over two years, grew withdrawn, defensive, and uncivil, but to only me, his mother.

The change began after his triumphant purchase of an electronic gaming system with the money he earned from mowing grass.

The two years that followed found him exhausting excessive time in the toxic milieu of the online gaming environment to the exclusion of other interests.

But my futile attempts to regulate his gaming time ensnared our relationship in an escalating power struggle.

From each toward the other, passive defiance, hostile antagonism, and angry outbursts defined our relationship. Under the duress of our strained dynamic, Devin raised an icy rampart of defense against me, a fortress that forbade any hint of meaningful communication between us.

Suppose Devin could find a healthier passion instead of gaming, I thought. He might find fulfillment in the abundance of life instead of the self-absorption of gaming and thereby restore our relationship.

At a loss to help Devin or to restore our relationship, I began another 24-Glory Be novena on June 9. "Look over Devin and protect him from the beast of self-absorption," I petitioned the Saint of the Child Jesus.

"And please ask the Holy Spirit to reveal to Devin the gifts God has given him so that he may know the joy of glorifying God through sharing his talents with others.

Finally, help me show kindness, gentleness, patience, and love in all my interactions with Devin."

I reassured The Little Flower that a rose was unnecessary to let me know she heard my petitions, but a simple sign of grace would do.

So, I finished the novena on June 7 and, as is the practice of my private prayer life, made no one privy to my petitions.

Two weeks later, my nurse friend, Marsha, invited me to lunch. As I approached the table where she awaited me, I gasped in astonishment:

Upon the table sat a breathtaking bouquet of six long-stemmed white roses—full, fragrant, linen-white buds, artfully arranged amid delicate clusters of baby's breath and graceful arcs of greenery.

"These are for you," my friend chirped, beaming.

"What's the occasion?" I replied, my eyes wide with awe.

"Your birthday last week," she remarked. "When you told me about receiving a white rose at church a while back, I figured you would like white roses for your birthday."

Marsha and I met as new nursing staff at Mercy Hospital. She was the first one I called to share my astounding story of receiving a white rose at church five days after starting my novena in May.

Yet, I never shared that my rose from Jesus Sun of Justice Church was my first in nearly four decades. Nor did I share that I prayed another novena in June.

I slid into the booth and revealed to her my petition to St. Thérèse. Together, we marveled at Providence and the presence of God in all human matters.

For two weeks, the lovely bouquet adorned my desk at home. And each time I glanced upon the splendid roses, I intuited the fragrant gift as a sign of spiritual friendship from my patron saint, St. Thérèse.

As the weeks passed, I saw answers to my prayers for Devin. With the help of St. Thérèse, I sought to enfold with kindness, gentleness, patience, and love each interaction with my defiant teenage son.

But alas! With each passing day, the ice between us began to melt.

The week after I finished my Novena, Devin, on his own accord, began opting to spend time with respectful friends instead of in the toxic milieu of online gaming.

Of his own volition, he started the diligent practice of his flute, and now two weeks into the new school year, he proclaims participation in marching band as his favorite activity.

My hope springs afresh that the work of the Holy Spirit reveals to Devin what may be the charism of music.

But, alas, I give a nod of confidence to my spiritual companion, St. Thérèse, that I have no doubt God listens to The Little Flower's intercessions for me and my petitions.

God is good!

To: Marise Gallica

From: Theodore Locherbie

Subject: Remarks–"A Shower of Roses"

Marise,

Your story, "A Shower of Roses," reflects what I can only describe as a host of "God-winks" (a personal experience of a coincidence so astonishing that one can perceive it as a sign of divine intervention, especially when perceived as the answer to a prayer).

Not being of the Catholic faith tradition, I'm unfamiliar with an intercessory prayer to the saints.

Nonetheless, your account of your God-winks held me spellbound: the figurative "rose" of kind words from your supervisor, the spiritual "rose" of encouragement while praying in the Chapel, and the white rose bouquet from your nurse friend.

What a marvelous host of coincidences for any person to experience! Your openness to "signs" as messages from your saint might inspire others to "see" signs they are on the right path.

More so, the anguish you portray at expressing disclosure gone unfavorably and the despair at finding no words to process such an emotional experience may resonate with readers who have had similar experiences, especially persons who use writing to process difficult emotions.

I am intrigued to see how the "path" on which your "God-winks" lead you will unfold through your creative expression of writing.

Regards, Theodore Locherbie

To: Theodore Locherbie

From: Marise Gallica

Subject: Remarks–"A Shower of Roses"

Mr. Locherbie,

Thank you for your kind remarks. I, too, revere the synchronicities I've experienced through petitions to The Little Flower.

No doubt, countless Catholics attest to the intercessory power of the saints. But all persons may seek intercession from saints, no matter their faith tradition.

Catholics believe that saints cooperate with God through their prayers. So, likewise, graces are from God, and through the intercession of saints, God blesses those who seek the truth.

Regards, Marise

Chapter 7 The Bread of Life

To: Theodore Locherbie

From: Marise Gallica

Subject: "The Bread of Life"

Hello Mr. Locherbie,

Attached is my next chapter, "The Bread of Life." I meant to complete it in time for you to review it over your holiday break. But putting to paper this narrative was mentally and emotionally challenging.

Thank you for agreeing to read my story over your holiday break.

Regards, Marise

Dear St. Thérèse,

This narrative, "The Bread of Life," reflects the most tumultuous yet mystifying and beautiful interior period of my adult life.

Returning to my Catholic faith three years ago, I prayed to God to transform me. And within days of my prayer, the landscape of my interior life began to shift.

Little did I realize that the heart of that transformation called for examining who and what I believed myself to be.

Hence, "The Bread of Life" portrays what may be the beginning of my spiritual awakening.

In friendship, Marise

The Bread of Life

The Belief

Six weeks passed since I put "Laetare Sunday" to rest, a story I hoped writing and sharing would restore me to my old self. That endeavor proved fruitless.

It was the middle of July, but I had yet to begin the ambitious personal projects I set forth to renew at the start of summer break. Sadly, my garden bed lay untended. My piano practice stalled. And my weekly running regimen halted.

In the months since I shared "Laetare Sunday," I suffered dullness of mind, laxity of concentration, slowness of energy, and staleness of joy. Something in my universe was out of order, but I could not name its source.

Unable to navigate out of my unrest, I began another novena to St. Thérèse on Monday morning, July 9.

"Please help me find my way out of this disquietude in my soul," I pleaded to my patron saint.

"I can find neither the source nor the end of my unrest. My faith is parched, and I thirst for your spiritual companionship."

That afternoon, preparing for its grand opening the next day, the hospital held a reception for eighty potential referral agencies.

As a member of the hospital's leadership team, I circulated among the visitors, making small talk and promoting the hospital with the guests, the last of whom was a middle-aged man representing an agency.

The encounter appeared harmless, but his remark left me unsettled.

Later that evening, I turned my attention to revising my journal story, "David's Brick," which I planned to submit for publication in a popular Catholic faith magazine.

I was confident that it was a well-written narrative depicting spiritual insight and that it was not overly personal.

In fact, the previous month's edition featured a personal narrative by a college student describing how he conquered his porn addiction. I applauded the young man's courage for what could be more personal than disclosing a porn addiction in a national publication!

Indeed, I mused my story wasn't overly personal compared to his.

I submitted my story on Thursday that week, anticipating a response weeks later. Instead, the magazine rejected my work the following day.

So dejected, I could only conclude that so trite and meaningless was my story that I couldn't even compete with the confessions of a porn addict.

My caustic inner critic confirmed my conclusion. "Shame on you for believing your story would be accepted," my ever-present critic hissed. "Your story is insignificant and irrelevant. No one wants to hear your story!"

Numb with the sting of rejection from the magazine, superimposed over the unsettling encounter with the reception guest earlier that week, I drifted through the rest of the week wishing I were invisible.

That Sunday, I attended Mass at a rural Catholic church in the next county. The stinging rejection of my story and the unsettling encounter with the reception guest made it an emotionally trying week.

No doubt I wanted to go to Mass, where no one knew me, where I could be "invisible." But later that day, my older son, Julian, called to chat.

"It happened again," I said, heaving a sigh of resignation. "During the hospital's open house last week, I was making standard business small talk with a guest, and within three sentences, he mentions '...my wife....'"

"Why is it," I continued with an edge in my voice, "whenever I make small talk with men, no matter the setting, they always throw that '...my wife...' or '...my girlfriend...' statement out there, right up front?"

I'm neither flirting nor interested, so why the compulsion to dispel any doubt about attachment status?"

"Maybe it's because you're beautiful," my son posited.

"That can't be it," I countered. "If I were beautiful, people would've told me as much."

He asserted, "Most women are flattered at the suggestion. Perhaps you've had a thousand affirmations but never received them all these years."

"But I'm not beautiful!" I protested. "If I were beautiful, I could've competed in the pair-bonding market years ago," I yelled, my voice reaching a fever pitch.

"If I were beautiful, I wouldn't need a thousand affirmations!" I cried as my phone slipped from my trembling hands onto the floor. I stopped to catch my breath.

"Julian? Are ... are you still there?" I stuttered, fumbling with my smartphone in my sweaty palms.

"Yes?" he responded in a low, quiet voice.

An awkward silence ensued, and then my son finally spoke.

"Mom, think about what just happened, not what you said, but what you felt in your body."

I paused and then recounted my reaction to the suggestion that I might be beautiful. My heart pounded, and my hands trembled.

"Umm... so.... Why is my reaction relevant?" I queried.

"I challenged a core belief about yourself," Julian stated in his signature, matter-of-fact tone.

"Your ego perceived that challenge as a threat, and your primitive brain mounted a defense reaction no different than were you chased by a lion."

"What do you mean by 'core belief'?" I inquired.

My son explained that your core beliefs form how you think and see yourself. Your core beliefs are formed in childhood and are based on your memories, impressions, and sensations.

Core beliefs form the basis of the ego, the mask or persona each person wears as one's identity to the outside world. Therefore, the ego perceives any challenge to its core beliefs as a threat to that identity.

"Mother, you have a core belief that you're not beautiful, so your ego fights or flees any challenge to that belief," my son said, his voice laced with compassion.

"It wouldn't matter if you receive a thousand affirmations that you're beautiful. Your ego interprets any affirmation as an assault on its identity."

I sat silently, tears pooling in my eyes.

"Most people live their whole lives believing the mask they wear is who they really are," Julian continued.

"But the ego is only a false identity constructed from the stories we tell ourselves based on what others say we are."

"Your core belief goes deeper than believing you're not beautiful," he added.

"Your core beliefs might be worth examining to see if they apply to who you are or who you want to become," he remarked reassuringly.

We issued cordial goodbyes, and for the rest of the day, I pursued any number of distractions to avoid dwelling on our conversation. But that night, I slept fitfully, unable to escape my son's penetrating insight.

Until that day, I'd never heard of core beliefs. The revelation that a core belief wielded inestimable power over my physical, cognitive, and emotive reflexes rendered me stultified. I needed time and space to absorb what it meant.

The Toxin

I called in sick to work the following day. I went to the Adoration Chapel to make my novena prayers to The Little Flower, where I pleaded another entreaty.

"In the months since I shared my highway story with Fr. Pepe, my soul has known nothing but unrest," I prayed.

"And now, this notion of core beliefs and ego identity renders me lost. I have no idea what ego identity means or how to identify and change my core beliefs. So I want to return to who I was before I sent that blasted letter to Fr. Pepe."

Through the chapel windows, I gazed at clouds adrift in the brilliant summer sky and intuited... nothing but silence. But sadly, my spiritual companion, St. Thérèse, a reliable presence in my trials lately, seemed conspicuously absent that day.

Despairing, I closed my eyes and contemplated the encounter with the reception guest. Rationally, I suspected the man did what any upstanding man does upon encountering a female. He consciously or unconsciously puts up a "hedge" to protect his relationship with his significant other.

Throughout my adult life, such hedges were barely a blip in my subconscious. Why the distress now, I pondered.

My son's words echoed in my mind: "It's because you're beautiful. Most women feel flattered at the suggestion."

With that, a hot flush of shame engulfed me. I was alone in the Chapel before only God, yet it was the same wave of shame I experienced following my encounter with the reception guest.

My primal instinct impelled me to flee the toxic rush of shame. But my higher-order brain overruled the impulse, for why run from complicated feelings in the merciful presence of the Holy Eucharist.

I stayed with the shame that hour and shuffled through the countless memories, experiences, and beliefs that make me who I am.

That hour of reflection revealed that messages subtle and overt from childhood skewed my view about who I am.

I left the Chapel anxious for a sign from The Little Flower to acknowledge my prayers. But then, I sternly reminded myself that compared to the pressing needs of others, my needs are insignificant.

I shouldn't pester my patron saint, I chided. A famous saint like St. Thérèse has more pressing requests to intercede.

So, I decided to faithfully continue my regular Chapel visits, but nonetheless, stop hoping for signs my saint heard my prayers.

The Joker

Over the next few weeks, I undertook a self-directed crash course on ego, identity, and core beliefs through countless Internet resources. What I discovered was telling about my opinions about myself and how I saw myself.

I recollected how I yearned to be beautiful when I was a girl, as do typical pre-teen and teenage girls. But that desire was met with piercing sibling and maternal mockery throughout those years.

Implicit was that to be beautiful was to invite shameful character traits—vanity, conceit, arrogance, selfishness, and superficiality—unsavory character traits worthy of shame for which I feared my family would ostracize me.

The youngest of a large family, I was vulnerable to the approval and disapproval of my mother and siblings. I thus interpreted the family myth that being attractive is shameful.

To cope, my ego – and likewise, the persona that I presented to the outside world—crafted the tale that I cannot be beautiful lest I risk condemnation by my family.

My ego dutifully adopted that narrative, and with my continual retelling of that story over time, my ego spun that yarn into the powerful core belief of shame. Yet, sadly, forty years later, my ego fiercely guarded that makeshift story.

Yet of the countless cards that make me who I am, my ego was nothing but the Joker in my deck. A card of no value that in traditional decks substitutes for a missing card, the Joker in my deck was my false identity of shame.

A card whose value a lifetime ago was to preserve a sense of belonging for a sensitive, vulnerable child, it was now a card whose value had long since expired.

One evening near the end of July, while contemplating in the Chapel, I recalled my desperate pleas to the Little Flower three weeks before:

"Please help me find my way out of this disquietude in my soul. I can find neither the source nor the end of my unrest."

So, I mused to myself that I had yet to see a sign my saint heard my prayer. Nonetheless, at least I'd discovered my core belief of shame.

My core belief of shame wielded the greatest dominion over whom and what I believed myself to be.

Shame shadowed my perception of the reception guest's encounter, and shame tarred my response to the magazine's rejection of my story.

Shame hobbled my motivation to write "Laetare Sunday," and shame tormented my self-disclosures described in that story.

And finally, I realized that shame choked my joy of creative expression through writing. But, alas! My reflection revealed the source of my unrest.

Despite what I believed was a nod of confidence from St. Thérèse in the sign of a white rose to share "Laetare Sunday," my ego perceived that affirmation as a threat.

To preserve its false identity, my ego cast a mortifying pall of shame over my joy of writing after I shared the story and continued to do so two months later.

The distressing events earlier in the month were signs that The Little Flower interceded for me as Providence turned over three clues to help me find my way.

The reception guest encounter called forth shame at the expression of my physical self, a belief deflected into my subconscious since middle school.

Likewise, the rejection of my story provoked shame at my creative expression of self through writing, a view that shades how I perceive my connection with others.

Finally, my son's penetrating insight invited me to examine how disharmony of core beliefs, ego, and identity creates discord in my soul. These signs all occurred within days of starting my novena and pointed to the recurring theme of shame.

I bowed my head and cracked a humble smile. I envisioned the nearby presence of The Little Flower, my spiritual companion, and her gaze pouring unconditional love upon me as if to say, "You see, Marise, my dear friend? God always provides the signs you need if you have the faith to see them."

I could not return to who I was before I sent my highway narrative to Fr. Pepe. My soul could not subsist indefinitely under a false identity of shame. So, I prayed for the fortitude to penetrate my core belief and expose the root of my shame.

The Wound

My self-directed study of ego and identity led to an examination of my core wound. That wound is shame, the profoundly painful belief that I am irredeemably flawed and unworthy of love, fulfillment, connection, and belonging.

Indeed, the wounding shame I experienced as a child sculpted my false identity and shaded my core beliefs about myself.

As a young child, I didn't recognize shame. In my worldview, my mother treated each of her children with equanimity. I believed I was a beloved, joyful girl who was no less and no more than my siblings in my mother's eyes.

That belief fractured in July 1973 after I turned nine.

I was in my second season of competing on the local swim team. That summer, I qualified for the district swim meet. Five other teammates also qualified for the meet, where we would compete against swimmers representing large, year-round clubs from surrounding states.

Given that we were a small, seasonal team, the local media deemed our qualifying for the meet quite the feat. The team arranged for us six swimmers to be interviewed on a local noontime TV news show.

My teammates and I arrived at the station shortly before noon. Without preparation, we were shuffled into the studio, lined up in a group, taller ones in the back, shorter ones in front (that included me). Then live recording began.

After the host's brief introduction, the camera pointed at me, whereby the host inquired, "In which event will you be swimming?"

Under the hot intrusive glare of the studio lights, I cast my bashful brown eyes downward, dumbfounded with stage fright.

"Um... I swim in the nine and ten age group," I finally mumbled into the mic in front of me, at which the brunette host giggled politely and moved to the next swimmer.

On the ride home, I heard nothing but silence. I fidgeted in my seat, wondering about my response to the host. My mother, who was driving, spoke not a word, which led me to believe nothing was wrong. So, I thought nothing more of the interview and spent a carefree day at the pool.

That night, with my pixie haircut still wet from swimming, I cheerfully joined my siblings and parents at the family dinner table. With a twinkle in his eyes, my father peered over at me and inquired about the news show.

"That Marise should be ashamed of herself!" my mother retorted from across the table, her voice caustic with shame. "How could she be so dumb!" she continued as if I weren't there. "It wasn't a hard question. All Marise had to do was answer a simple question."

All fell silent around the table. I sat motionless, immobilized by the paralytic toxin of shame, amplified by the unanticipated humiliation of maternal scorn in front of my family. I fought back the tears.

Her relentless rant continued through dinner.

Per my mother's dinnertime rule, children were not allowed to leave the table until everyone finished eating. So, I stayed in the pillory, where I absorbed the shame of my mother's dehumanizing diatribe of sarcasm, hostility, disdain, and disgust.

No one around the table spoke in my defense, and no one circled back later to offer support or affirmation.

That night the freshly gored wound of shame began to embed the painful belief that I'm inherently unworthy of love and connection. To a child, my family's silence at the table signaled that I deserved the scorn; their abandonment after dinner felt as if I were unworthy of belonging.

To assert that a single bout of irrational parenting forever changed my view of myself might be presumptuous. But that episode spawned a cascade of beliefs that embedded my shame into a deep-seated core belief.

My mother never sought to salve the wound after the incident. On the contrary, that want of connection fractured my belief that I was worthy of love and a relationship.

To salvage my standing with her, I tried to stay invisible, for no attention was more tolerable than negative attention. Thus, shame became the veil behind which I hid my authentic self.

Fear of shame displaced my triumphant exuberance for life with the restraint of self-conscious inhibition. That fear manifested within days. At the district meet the following week, I was so self-conscious that I choked during the race.

I placed dead last, despite having the fastest entry time in the heat. My mother never commented on the race, and I could only conclude that my disappointing finish was another cause for shame.

From age nine onward, I stopped sharing my victories and challenges because I feared the shaming by my mother and siblings. I stopped asking for help and stopped voicing my needs. For a young child with no recognizable allies, it was my only strategy for feeling like I belonged.

Ironically, my mother and siblings never seemed to notice that I became invisible as time passed. Compared to my siblings and their celebrated academic, athletic, social, and career achievements, mine were unremarkable.

Compared to their personal trials and triumphs, mine, too, were insignificant. So, I could only conclude that I didn't matter.

Over the next forty-five years, my core wound grew more intrusive with beliefs corroborating my identity of shame: I'm not attractive. I'm not enough. I'm too sensitive. I'm a burden. I'm needy. I don't matter. I'm not important. I'm broken. I'm irredeemably flawed. I'm unworthy of love and connection.

If there was evidence that those beliefs were untrue, it was either inconsistent or untrustworthy, or never forthcoming, or my Joker ego denied it.

Shame in hues subtle and bold colored every card in the deck of whom I believed myself to be. The leitmotif of my life, my core belief of shame, stained all that I was, all I did, and all I would ever be.

In Persona Christi

Two days later, I attended early Sunday Mass at Jesus Sun of Justice Church. That week's Gospel spoke of Jesus exhorting the crowd to fixate not on bread as physical nourishment but to associate God's gift of his son Jesus as the eternal Bread of Life.

"When we receive Holy Communion as a token symbol of Jesus' flesh, it's merely bread," Fr. Pepe proclaimed in his homily that day. "But when we believe it's the true flesh of Jesus, the eternal Bread of Life, the Holy Eucharist transforms us."

Although the Gospel of the woman at the well was not that day's reading, as Mass proceeded, I could only contemplate the Samaritan woman and her dialog with Jesus at the well.

Jesus saw the woman not as a "sinner" but as a wounded child hiding behind her false identity of shame. So he enjoined the woman to leave at the well her false identity, a faded jar of shame filled with makeshift stories from her brokenness. In its place, he would fill her with her true self, the identity of a beloved child of God.

The woman grasped the transformative power of Christ while he sat with her at the well in the midday desert heat. So, that day, she courageously shed her false identity of shame and embraced her authentic self as a child of God.

I fixed my eyes upon the crucifix above the altar. But, alas! I finally grasped the profound meaning of the transformative power of the Holy Eucharist:

During a quiet weeknight Mass at Jesus Sun of Justice Church a year ago, God's gift of Jesus, the eternal Bread of Life, met me, too, "at the well."

When the priest, acting in persona Christi, reached out to me as I received the Holy Eucharist that night, my soul saw Jesus reaching out to me and saying, "Woman, you needn't hide your true self behind a false identity of shame."

Yet so entrenched was my identity of unworthiness that my Joker ego repulsed with a flinch the merciful, affirming touch of Christ.

It's human nature to feel ashamed of shame. So we run; we hide from shame, as did I for the better part of a year.

My missive to Fr. Pepe, my letter, was but a means to deny and deflect my mortifying pall of shame—my flinch of shame, my shame of shame, my identity of shame.

Yet through an interior journey that led to a deeper understanding of my false identity, I finally understood the transformative power of the Eucharist as the eternal Bread of Life.

I turned my gaze to the pews around me. The congregation was filing toward the altar for Holy Communion, and I arose to join the line.

I approached the altar, and with cupped hands, I accepted not a wafer of bread from a silver ciborium but the Bread of Life from the gift of God, the nourishment I would need for the transformative journey to my true self.

No one proclaims the purgative stage to be easy or painless. Indeed, putting this narrative into words demanded the courage to sit with painful emotions in recollecting long-repressed wounds.

Bringing those recollections to life on paper commanded the discipline to relive the deep wounding of difficult memories in vivid color.

Nonetheless, composing this narrative was purgative, for in doing so, I arrived at a new perspective on my role in my family as the "invisible" child.

A role associated with families of addiction, the invisible child seeks safety from the chaos by staying out of the fray and unseen.

My father was an alcoholic. I knew my father drank, but he was never unkind or harsh to me. Instead, we shared a good father-daughter relationship.

In fact, I believed I was his favorite; he always gazed at me with a twinkle in his eyes, even as he lay upon his hospice bed at age eighty-four in the fog of advanced Alzheimer's disease and the pain of terminal cancer.

I never considered how my father's alcoholism affected me. Yet, through exploring the roots of my shame in composing this story, I realized the shame I absorbed in the shadow of his cross of addiction.

My father's drinking affected me because it affected my mother's relationship with me. That change in our relationship started in 1973 when I incurred my core wound.

Earlier that year, my father, a physician, lost his job at the hospital. It was months before he would find work again. I would learn years later that his employer caught him drinking on the job.

Months later, one of my older sisters, who attended a local Catholic high school, overdosed at school while my parents were out of town at a physician's conference.

She was rushed to the hospital by ambulance, accompanied by the school's priest chaplain, who stayed with her at the hospital while my parents flew home on an emergency flight.

My sister survived, but I would only learn of the ordeal decades later.

My father's drinking continued for years, as did my mother's codependency. So, my immediate family circle fell into two camps: those who required my mother to run interference to hide the shame of addiction and those who brought pride to the family through remarkable academic, athletic, and career achievements.

I fell into neither camp. I speculate that my mother's codependency drained her emotional, mental, physical, and spiritual energy, and she had nothing left to give to others.

I can only imagine my mother's cross of shame was as heavy as my father's cross of addiction. Yet, through composing this narrative, I am overwhelmed with forgiveness, compassion, mercy, and love for my mother and father, who each gave their best to raise my siblings and me.

God is good!

To: Marise Gallica

From: Theodore Locherbie

Subject: Remarks—"Bread of Life"

Marise,

Upon finishing your "Bread of Life" story, a host of words flowed forth instantaneously: honest, revealing, vulnerable, insightful, helpful, exposed, powerful, valuable, courageous, spiritual, encouraging, and probing.

With your experiences and reflections, your story will remind readers of the wounds of shame and self-condemnation they carry. Indeed, your account may serve to move your readers to peel back layers of scar tissue to discover the root of their pain.

More so, your narrative reminds your readers that, like the woman at the well, they, too, can find spiritual and personal healing on the path to finding peace, joy, and self-value in their lives.

I appreciate your insight "It's human nature to feel ashamed of shame!" Haven't we all felt ashamed over something we did and then experienced the shame of being shamed?

Moreover, your summary concisely encapsulates your personal story thus far: how through "Divine Providence," you had undertaken an "interior journey" that gave you an understanding of the source of your "false identity" as well as the "transformative power of the Holy Eucharist." You need to publish this!

Regards, Theodore Locherbie

To: Theodore Locherbie

From: Marise Gallica

Subject: Re: Remarks–"The Bread of Life"

I'm glad that my narrative might make for a poignant story! But, of course, I prefer to read biographies over fiction. Indeed, I would never attempt to author a novel, especially as a new author.

Nonetheless, I've shared my narratives with my son, Julian, whom, you might recall, was a student in your Honors English class ten years ago.

Julian pointed out that my story parallels the archetypes and events of the "Hero's Journey" monomyth, a narrative pattern common to myths and stories across all cultures and eras of the human experience.

I didn't set out to craft my story to match the monomyth schema of the Hero's Journey with the various character archetypes and transformative stages. But my story is unfolding that way!

Regards, Marise

To: Marise Gallica

From: Theodore Locherbie

Subject: Remarks–"The Bread of Life"

Marise,

My interest is piqued by how your story's parallel to the hero's journey will clearly emerge by the conclusion of your writing.

May I suggest that your narrative reveal the positive changes and benefits you've realized since your journey into your psyche?

Your insights, new spiritual awareness, and connections may resonate with readers who can identify with your story.

Moreover, sharing your reflections will give readers hope that they can also find closure and peace by discovering the source of the wounds they have experienced.

Regards, Theodore Locherbie

Chapter 8 The Metanoia

To: Theodore Locherbie

    From: Marise Gallica

    Subject: Writer's block

    Hello Mr. Locherbie,

    I hope you're having a restful summer break. I planned to send you my next chapter, "The Metanoia," at the start of summer to allow you time to review it before school begins.

    Unfortunately, I've not progressed on this chapter since last winter when my motivation to write ran aground in the quicksand of writer's block.

    Regards, Marise

To: Marise Gallica

    From: Theodore Locherbie

    Subject: Remarks—Writer's Block

    Marise,

    I like what you've developed in your chapters thus far. I'm intrigued by how your "journey" will unfold. I know you will arrive at a meaningful, inspiring, and personal narrative once you "melt" your writer's block.

    Regards, Theodore Locherbie

To: Theodore Locherbie

    From: Marise Gallica

    Subject: My writing style

    Hello Mr. Locherbie,

Thank you for your encouragement. I attribute my writer's block to the wounding assessment by a reader in my trusted circle who, upon reading my Bread of Life narrative, declared my journal entries and writing style to be nothing more than "sentimental fluff!"

Indeed, I've recently read several writing blogs addressing "sentimentality, or excessively 'saccharine' writing.

The bloggers contend that sentimentality renders a work shallow. Does my writing style come across as sentimental?

Note that this reader in my trusted "circle" makes no claim to being a literary critic. But she is a college graduate with substantial life experience and an avid reader. So, does my writing style strike you as overly sentimental?

I would appreciate your candid insight.

Regards, Marise

To: Marise Gallica

    From: Theodore Locherbie

    Subject: Your writing style

    Marise,

Go ahead and send me your next chapter when you are finished, as I will send my remarks after I finish grading papers.

Concerning sentimentality in your writing, I've never seen this to be an issue in your stories. In fact, your writing style uses a variety of voices and styles, which gives effective variance and interest throughout your compositions.

At times you have captured the beauty of nature and connected this to your present or past life experiences.

At times you have been vulnerable in exposing the personal and theological struggles that have haunted you, including those from your family upbringing, which has impacted you to this day.

You have been vulnerable in revealing the conflicts you've faced and the decisions you've made concerning your relationship with Carl.

Likewise, you have been vulnerable in wrestling with self-esteem issues that, so too, women struggle with in finding value in themselves and in their lives.

You've been vulnerable in sharing your faith and God's mysteries revealed through the flowers and birds in nature and in times of quiet reflection when you see His revelations.

Suppose a reader deems your insights and stories "sentimental." Such an assessment is favorable, given that you've developed a cohesive collection of compelling stories with reflective insights.

Indeed, you need to share your narratives; your readers might appreciate and learn from your sharing them.

Moreover, your chapter may reveal fresh and thought-provoking insight to your readers!

Regards, Theodore Locherbie

To: Theodore Locherbie

    From: Marise Gallica

    Subject: My writing style

    Hi Mr. Locherbie,

    I've finally finished my long-fought narrative, "The Metanoia."

    The title derives from the Greek "metanoien," which means a spiritual change of heart or casting off of one's false identities through what is often described as a transformational period of one's life, accompanied by doubt, fear, and a lost sense of purpose.

Indeed, my story may resonate with countless readers, especially those who, only in late middle age, begin to realize the influence one's family of origin bears on a person's long-held belief about themself.

My gratitude, Mr. Locherbie, for your affirmation and encouragement. I am beyond grateful for the time you so generously give as my writing mentor.

Regards, Marise

Dear St. Thérèse,

My gratitude for the blessing of your spiritual companionship. Sharing deeply personal narratives of one's life can be difficult.

I cherish your spiritual presence in my sharing. Indeed, the sacred is the gift of presence, as I hope my narrative, "The Metanoia," portrays.

In friendship, Marise

The Metanoia

The Piñata

Nourished by the gift of the Holy Eucharist at Mass, I set forth the next day to discover my authentic self.

That day, I met for the first time with April, a therapist with whom I had booked an appointment earlier in the summer.

Bewildered at Carl's frequent refrain to "get my head fixed," I finally elected to seek therapy. My sister, Marla, a family law attorney, recommended April.

"She's one of the best!" she assured me after I casually inquired if she knew of a good therapist.

But unbeknownst to me when I scheduled the appointment, the intervening weeks found me unearthing my core belief of shame identity.

So, I arrived for my first appointment hopeful that therapy could help me reconfigure my core belief, which thereby might improve my marriage.

"My marriage is a failure, and Carl faults me...." I began....

"He boasts that he's trustworthy because he never lies," I bemoaned toward the end of the hour. "But I can't trust him with my feelings.

"Every time I risk emotional vulnerability, he ignores, invalidates, or rebuffs me," I barked in the harsh voice of a woman scarred by scorn.

"How come everyone else gets chosen as someone's special 'other,' but I don't?" I cried in a raised voice, grasping my smudged eyeglasses from my face and flinging my arm across the couch in exasperation.

My eyeglasses flew airborne, landing with a thud on the carpet.

"Try to keep it down; the walls are thin," April whispered.

"Sorry," I mumbled, throwing her an apologetic glance as I scooped my glasses off the floor.

"Most of my clients have similar issues," April remarked. 'You deserve a fulfilling relationship. So we'll work on that."

I departed my first appointment, optimistic that she would help me plumb the depths of my shame identity and emerge with a healthier sense of self.

But six weeks and five sessions later, April never allowed me to discuss significant experiences of family and other relationships.

Thus, each time I broached the subject of my shame identity, the therapist deflected, dodged, or redirected the discussion.

"We can't dwell in the past," April finally stated firmly. "We need to move forward."

Dismayed, I silently questioned her approach. But she was a licensed therapist with twenty-five years of experience, so I trusted her credentials.

I voiced my dissatisfaction to my son, Julian.

"I need the compassionate presence of a mental health professional to help me make sense of my core wound," I confided later that night to Julian. "But I can't get what I need from my therapist."

"That might be from never knowing where you stood with Grandma (my mother)," Julian conjectured. "Being unable to express your needs has probably been your default setting your whole life," he added.

Until my son's conjecture that day, I was blind to parallels between growing up in a relationship of uncertain status with my mother and being unable to express my needs as an adult.

At my next appointment, I eagerly suggested that we explore how my relationship with my mother shaped my core belief, at which April's face flushed red with anger.

I paused in tense silence, befuddled at what might've offended her. She finally spoke.

"I'm done!" she snapped. "I am not prepared to provide the scope of therapy you need!

"At your first appointment, you got so angry I was scared for my life!" she rasped with ire, jabbing her index finger in the air at me. "I don't feel safe with you!"

Then, dropping all pretense of a professional mask, she assailed me for my "brokenness." I sat dumbstruck amidst the verbal daggers hurling at me, aghast at the therapist's flagrant violation to "first do no harm," the unspoken oath of all human services professions.

Had I not possessed a modicum of mental stability, the diatribe might've pummeled me with shame and humiliation.

But, instead, I waxed bemused at the irrational outburst, for the therapist's ire felt no more threatening than watching a blindfolded child battering a pinata at a party.

My face twitched into a smirk, at which my assailant suddenly fell silent, spun her chair with her back to me, and thereby acknowledged my presence no further.

Upon completing the client termination form, April pointed out where to sign and gestured me out the door with neither eye contact nor words.

I departed unflapped by the lunacy of the unhinged therapist but dismayed that help was never forthcoming.

So, instead of therapy to help me heal my childhood wounds, I pondered that I perhaps needed spiritual direction to help me find God in my marriage.

The Direction

The next day, I explored a list of local Catholic spiritual directors, for who might be more qualified to help me find God in my marriage than one steeped in the theology of my faith?

I contacted three prospects twice over the next two weeks. But after my queries yielded no response, I abandoned my quest for spiritual direction.

On a Saturday evening in late autumn, despairing at my marriage gone inert, my therapy gone wayward, and my knock gone unanswered at the door of spiritual direction, I sought inspiration from the book, *"The Sacrament of the Present Moment."*

Penned in the 1700s by the Jesuit Rev. Jean-Pierre de Caussade, the book proclaims to "...help you learn to hear and understand when God speaks to you."

I'd read only the first chapter months before. But, as St. Thérèse was wont to do when seeking inspiration, I thus "... held the book and let fall open the pages to where Divine Providence would lead me."

My eyes were drawn to page thirty-nine:

> *"...God combats all personal affections of the soul... such as some path or way or by the guidance of some particular person. God upsets its plans and allows it to find nothing but confusion, trouble, emptiness, and folly. Hardly is it said that 'I must go this way; I must consult this person....' But God immediately says the exact contrary...."*

Indeed, my soul sought the path of a blessed marriage, mental health therapy, and spiritual direction. But God said the exact contrary.

God upset all my plans and allowed me to find nothing but confusion, trouble, emptiness, and folly. Yet, which direction to trim my sail, my soul could not infer.

The following day as I headed into Mass at Jesus Sun of Justice Church, I spied a folder under my driver's seat. I groaned. The folder held my preliminary divorce papers from Carl, my spouse of two years.

The eighteen-page legal form I painstakingly completed months before required only his signature to initiate an uncontested divorce.

But for two months, the papers resided on my car's floorboard; each time I sought his signature, I found reason to delay. Despite the demise of our twenty-two-year relationship in the two years since we wed, my deliberative nature forbade a rash decision.

"Your marriage is inauthentic," my voice of reason admonished as I ambled into the church. "You need to move forward with the divorce."

My asp-like inner critic mocked the notion. "Why not give it a few more years?" the ever-present asp sneered. "Perhaps you'll learn to like your hollow gourd of a marriage."

I winced at the sardonic venom but more so at the stark truth that marriage to my children's father foresaw no plausible future. Mass was about to begin. I settled into a pew in the back, vowing to seek Carl's signature by the end of the week.

Fr. Pepe opened his homily that Sunday with remarks about his prison ministry. "When I offer pastoral care to the men, I pose three questions: Why are you here? Where are you going? And how will you get there?" he remarked.

I sank back into the pew and let the questions sink in.

How I got "here" into an inauthentic marriage, I knew full well. But where was I going and how I would go "there," my soul could not discern.

So, I dropped anchor and moved neither toward nor away from the dissolution of my marriage.

The Stairwell

With my marriage moored at inertia, I redirected my focus to drafting my next story, "The Bread of Life." A work of depth examining the roots of my shame identity, the composition consumed my free time throughout the holiday season and for weeks afterward.

I returned to work after the holiday break on Jan. 2. The date marked the birthday of St. Thérèse, and while commuting to work that day, I reflected on the saint's conversion.

A loving but difficult child whose innate sensitivity ruled her emotions, the saint's conversion occurred on Christmas Eve, 1887, in the stairwell of her home in Lisieux, France.

On that luminous night, the fourteen-year-old Thérèse returned from Midnight Mass with her father and sisters, eager to discover the presents in her shoes in the chimney corner.

Yet as she ascended the stairwell, she overheard her father grumble, "Fortunately, this will be the last year!"

The words pierced her heart, and her eyes flooded with tears.

But in an instant, Jesus flooded her heart with charity, and Thérèse commanded her tears to joy, restoring her father's cheerfulness.

That moment, Thérèse recounted in her autobiography, signified her conversion from childhood to adulthood. By the grace of charity in that instant, she discovered that true happiness lies in looking beyond her self-centered needs or desires to empty herself for others.

I interpreted the story as a poignant depiction of self-mastery through detachment from the need for validation.

I, too, wrestled with emotions ruled by innate sensitivity and the need for external validation. Yet the self-mastery of sensitivity, which Thérèse achieved as a teenager, eluded me.

Instead, I learned to veil overwhelming emotions to avert shame for being needy, burdensome, emotional, and unimportant. The practice rendered me a functioning adult in an abrasive world.

But for want of detachment, masking my emotions drove them inward to thunder across my interior landscape for days—or years—depending on the circumstance.

Ironically, my need for external validation seemed to lose grip after April assailed me. My final encounter with April signaled my own "stairwell" experience in mastering my emotions, I conjectured, albeit with a bit of smugness at achieving the feat on my own merit.

The Lexicon

I finished "The Bread of Life" two weeks later. Then, armored by my newfound spirit of detachment, I distributed the story to my trusted circle of six, which included two select siblings, Miriam and Marla.

Marla, the newest reader in my circle, eagerly expressed interest in seeing my stories after I extended the invitation. Although we weren't close growing up, we enjoyed sibling camaraderie as college roommates and summer lifeguards.

But that camaraderie ground to a halt one day in my twenties. Mired in the straits of the young adult singles world, I trusted Marla that day to lend an empathetic ear and meaningful insight into a problematic dating situation I faced.

But as I disclosed the circumstance, she suddenly interjected with disgust, "You're so needy!"

Taken aback, I nonchalantly dismissed my problem. But deep rent the shorn trust. Thus on that day, I fled our conversation and our relationship, for "needy" ranked the most detestable in my lexicon of shame.

To avert the scarlet letter of neediness, I limited contact with Marla to casual phone calls three times a year and shallow pleasantries at family gatherings.

But my occasional phone calls went unreturned, and our banal communication went unnoticed. As the years passed, I could only conclude I was insignificant to Marla.

That disconnection continued for decades until three years ago when Julian casually inquired about our relationship.

After I recounted the fallout from the decades-old incident, he enjoined me to restore the connection.

"What if she still thinks I'm needy?" I countered. "The emptiness of disconnection is far less onerous than the shame of neediness."

"That was twenty-five years ago!" he remarked incredulously. "You've changed, and so has Marla. You need to try to re-establish the relationship," he urged.

I finally agreed. I contacted Marla, and we visited that night. But unfortunately, she could not recall the dialog that led to our disconnection years ago.

But she apologized and conceded that motherhood and her demanding career competed for time to connect in the intervening years.

Indeed, the next few months saw frequent, meaningful communication between us, through which she voiced enthusiastic support for my intent to publish my work.

The Closet

Overjoyed at my renewed trust in Marla and optimistic about a favorable response, I sent her "The Bread of Life" on a Thursday night in early February.

But sadly, that optimism vaporized the following day upon receipt of an unanticipated text message:

> "I suggest you write whatever ails you and the dark experiences you feel and put them under your mattress!

> "Your perceptions of reality and experiences are yours and no one else's. So, write all you want, but stop being negative about Mom, Dad, and the rest of us!"

Stunned by the incendiary text, I instantly suspected that Marla shared my "Bread of Life" story with Marjorie—the fire-breathing sibling whom I never made privy to my stories.

With fingers quivering, I scrolled through the flaming text message:

"Funny, no one knows who you are talking about with a sibling drug overdose. And why would you write about Dad drinking?! How did his drinking affect YOU? ... And you should let that comment about your makeup go.

"You do not have the right to dig into your siblings' or parents' baggage! And it's not yours to share! If you publish those stories, everyone in town will shame you for trashing Mom and Dad because everybody knows our parents loved all their kids and worked hard to be good citizens.

"Instead of writing, why don't you discuss all this while looking in the mirror? That would be a start at moving on from your perception of an awful childhood!"

Beset by the searing text and shattering betrayal, I retreated in silence as the weekend unfolded in a blur of emotion.

I finally reached out to Marla late Sunday night. A tense dialog ensued.

Marla proclaimed never hearing of a sibling's overdose. Defending her betrayal, Marla declared that she verified the story with Marjorie, the self-appointed guardian of family secrets.

The latter knew nothing of our sister Marilyn's ordeal at the Catholic high school.

I paused, recalling that our three older siblings, Martha, Marilyn, and Miriam, attended the Catholic high school in the 1970s, whereas we, the younger siblings, attended local public schools.

Unfortunately, Martha, who suffered a severe stroke years ago and is cognitively impaired, could not confirm the story. But Miriam, from whom I learned of the ordeal, could attest to what happened at the school.

"I didn't mean to upset anyone," I replied thoughtfully. "I only learned of this story years ago from Miriam. I've always been the last to know family secrets – I thought everyone already knew."

"You need to check your facts!" Marla cried. "None of your sisters overdosed!

"Furthermore, Marjorie and I were at the dinner table that night after the swim team interview, and Mom never yelled at you," Marla spat. "It never happened; you're making it up!

"You always hated Mom, and now you make her sound like a monster!" she roared.

"I didn't hate Mom," I remarked in a hushed voice. "I only wanted her to like me, but I was never shiny enough to catch her eye – she only saw me whenever I fell short."

"Well!" Marla retorted. "Mom always took you shopping on your birthday, and she never took us!"

"You're too sensitive!" she barked. "Stop being so sentimental about the past and move on!"

"I apologize for writing about my unpleasant memories," I declared. "But I'd like to have an authentic relationship with my siblings. Now that we're adults, could we have a dialogue about our family dynamics and how they might've shaped us?"

A tense pause ensued, and then Marla finally spoke.

"You can't expect an authentic relationship with us if you're going to trash Mom and Dad," she pronounced with terse authority.

"They're dead and can't defend themselves. Marise, you're writing historical fiction, and I won't support you. And if you dare publish your stories, so help me, I'm going to ... to... ugh!" she grunted with abhorrence.

In the following days, I sought insight into my narrative from Marilyn, who neither confirmed nor denied the ordeal. Instead, opting not to hear my story, she kindly enjoined me to "...write all you want but keep your stories in a box in your closet."

Likewise, I attempted a dialog with Miriam but surrendered my effort when she voiced discomfort with my narrative.

Finally, in a blind quest for a meaningful connection with my hopelessly estranged spouse, I queried Carl for his thoughts on my siblings' reaction to my story. My query elicited a whisper of affirmation – and a roar of rebuke.

"You do have a way with words, Marise, but I don't like your stories!" Carl remarked. "You always make me the bad guy; now you want to blame your family for your problems?!

"No wonder they're mad!" he bellowed. "Keep your family and me out of your stories! Until then, I don't want to hear them!"

I floundered the rest of the week.

Despite daily meditation in Adoration, my soul found no relief from the staggering pain of betrayal, invalidation, dismissal, rebuke, and threats by those I thought I could trust.

The Poverty

I attended Mass the following Sunday, for which the Gospel was the Sermon on the Mount. But Fr. Pepe's homily that day was lost on me, so despondent was I at the antipathy my story wrought.

In despair at my tenuous ties to my siblings and my abysmal connection to my spouse, I hastened to the Adoration Chapel that night. Then, in the gray light of an overcast winter evening, I sat in solitude before the bronze tabernacle – and wept.

"All I've ever wanted, God, was to be safe, seen, understood, affirmed, and cherished by those I thought I could trust – my family or a special other," I prayed.

"But when I find the courage to be vulnerable, I meet with avoidance, dismissal, betrayal, invalidation, reproach. I can't even pay someone to sit with my vulnerability," I uttered, recalling the therapist's deflection and rebuke.

I sunk my head into my hands and reflected upon the lifelong parameters of conditional love and acceptance imposed by my mother, siblings, and spouse:

"You are seen only when you fall short."

"You are heard only when you bring pride to the family."

"You are understood only in your assigned role.

"You are affirmed only when your experience validates ours."

"You are safe only when you hide your vulnerability."

"You are accepted only if you don't stir our own vulnerability.

"Why am I so undeserving of love?" I prayed. "If I were worthy of love, I would've been loved by now.

"My whole life, I've sought nonjudgmental love and acceptance, but to no avail. So instead, I've sought relationships and marriage, conformance to family and connection with siblings, self-help, and mental health therapy.

"Then, when love and acceptance were not found, I tried to fill the void with school, career, motherhood, pets, hobbies, and all sorts of busyness.

"I thought my newfound armor of rational detachment would guard me against rejection and shame, God. But my armored self could not withstand the rebuke of my family and spouse.

"After a lifetime of a self-directed search for love and acceptance, connection and meaning, God, my efforts signify the monumental shame of my fundamental failure to connect."

I fixed my gaze upon the sealed tabernacle – as if awaiting the salve of an epiphany to flow forth from the Blessed Sacrament within.

And lo, in that instant, I intuited the Divinity of the Holy Eucharist, speaking to me in a timbre resonant with compassion.

"Marise, my precious child, sin means separation from God," whispered the Divine voice. "Your belief that you are unworthy of love separates you from God. Your attachment to your false identity of shame isolates you from love, for God *is* Love."

I sat motionless, absorbing the profoundly painful truth of my disordered belief of unworthiness.

Then, without provocation, the story of Moses and the burning bush surfaced in my contemplation.

But the passage called forth neither from my recent memory of Mass liturgy nor from my fund of favorite Bible passages; I never comprehended why God demanded Moses remove his sandals before approaching the bush.

I meditated on Moses and the animal-hide sandals bound to his feet with worn leather straps – humble footwear that spoke of his identity as a lowly shepherd, an identity assigned to him by his family.

"Marise," the Blessed Sacrament intimated, "unstrap your false identity of shame and leave it in the sand of the past.

"Fear not to approach me in the vulnerability of the true self I created you to be, Marise, for I have work I need to do in you and with you and through you."

"I can't do this myself," I whispered, choking with tears. "Only you can loosen the fetters of my false identity of shame," I pleaded. "Help me, God!"

I arose to depart, and upon bowing before the tabernacle, I recalled the words of Jesus from the Gospel that morning, "...Blessed are the poor in spirit, for theirs is the kingdom of heaven."

I paused in a thoughtful pose in the candle-lit Chapel, recalling the truth of the Gospel passage: Only through complete dependence on God could I shed my false identity of shame and unworthiness.

I departed the Chapel resigned to my helplessness but relieved of the hopelessness of transformation by my own devices.

The Presence

The following day commenced a routine work week. Resigned to letting God unbind the knots of my shame identity, I immersed myself in my work, directing my energy to my patients and coworkers.

But within days, I found my fortitude for workplace engagement flagging, so great was my distress at my spouse and siblings' antipathy toward my narrative.

Nonetheless, I faithfully continued my visits to the Adoration Chapel, seeking only the Divine Presence in the Holy Eucharist to sit with me in my pain, for I knew not which way to turn.

Then, one day in late February, I went to the bistro in the hospital lobby for a mid-afternoon cup of brew. At the coffee kiosk stood Lynette, a petite woman in her thirties who looked young enough to be my daughter.

The wife of an evangelical pastor and mother of two young children, she volunteered at the nursing home in the north wing of the hospital. Over the next few months, we frequently passed each other in the bistro, where we became workplace acquaintances.

"You seem a bit sad," she observed as we awaited fresh brew on a Friday afternoon in early spring.

"Umm ... family stuff," I muttered.

"Would you like to talk about it?" she queried.

I paused in careful reflection: Dare I disclose painful family drama, which might paint our future encounters socially awkward? Dare I risk vulnerability and rejection again?

"I journal to capture the interesting stories of my own life," I heard myself blurt in the hush of the bistro. "But a narrative I wrote recently about my childhood didn't go over so well with my siblings and spouse."

She cocked her eyebrow inquisitively, inviting me to share a bit more.

Then, with unanticipated emotion, out poured my "Bread of Life" story, the crushing sibling reaction, and the concomitant vortex of anguish in which I was drowning.

"I'm hurt that my siblings invalidated my experience growing up because my interpretation doesn't match theirs," I whispered.

"I'm taken aback that they take affront at my search for the truth of our family dynamics. I'm aggrieved that they contend I'm writing historical fiction that villainizes mom and defames the family.

"I feel misunderstood that Marla recalls only that mom took me, and not her, on birthday shopping sprees," I remarked wryly, "as if birthday shopping sprees define the gold standard of meaningful mother-daughter relationships.

"So, too, I feel dismissed that my siblings glibly deny years of mockery at my appearance under the falsehood that my pain stems from a one-time unfavorable comment from my mom about my makeup.

"I didn't need my mother's gift of presents from a birthday shopping spree," I uttered in desperation. "I needed the gift of her presence in the trials of growing up and moving through life."

Lynette nodded with rapt intrigue at my surging catharsis.

"I needed my mother's presence when I went out on the sixth round at the county spelling bee," I declared emphatically.

"I needed her presence when I struggled to pass algebra, when I fouled out for the twelfth game in a row, when I lost by half a stride at league track, and when I was overlooked for senior class awards.

"Even my moments of life-changing joy and meaning she dismissed and derided, such as when as an unwed mother, I chose life instead of abortion, and I decided to keep my baby instead of surrendering him for adoption.

"The truth is," I remarked, "my mother dismissed my victories and disregarded my disappointments, but she registered disdain in my every disgrace," I sputtered.

"Yet so ashamed was I of falling short that I fearfully guarded my countless other trials and more obscure pain.

Thus, I dared not disclose such moments to anyone, especially my mother, lest I risk being shamed for being too sensitive and needy."

"Would you like to share some of those moments?" Lynette queried in a voice steeped in kindness.

I cast my eyes downward in self-conscious regard.

"Umm ... there was that moment when:

"No one asked me to dance at my first school dance; I froze during my middle school piano contest solo; a teacher told me I was fat.

"There was that moment when:

"I didn't have a prom date; I had no one to walk with at graduation; I didn't fit in with my college sports team.

"There was that moment when:

"My first job out of college wasn't going well; a guy I really liked asked me out but then took his life two months after we met."

I halted and inhaled a deep breath and then glanced at Lynette, gazing at me with eyes pooled with tears.

We sat without words in shared silence, her kind face speaking empathy and compassion and my connection-starved soul absorbing her wholehearted acceptance and presence.

I finally broke the warm silence.

"The meaning of my 'Bread of Life' narrative lies not in discovering my shame identity through composing my story," I said, "but in confronting my shame identity after sharing it.

"My siblings' antipathy paralyzes me with shame," I sputtered. "I feel like a pariah, for none have contacted me for months, and I feel too vulnerable to reach out to them.

"I finally sent Marla an apology, but she never acknowledged my gesture to restore our relationship. I can only conclude that I deserve the shame."

Lynette returned a vexed gaze.

"Beyond the crushing shame from my siblings," I continued, "I'm ashamed, too, that only in late middle age am I finally processing the emotional poverty of my childhood.

"I'm ashamed that I grieve the wounds of a contentious relationship long past with my mother because our cultural narratives of motherhood dictate that grieving those wounds dishonors one's mother, who cannot defend herself in death.

"Worse, I'm ashamed that I still wince at the slights I suffered growing up, slights that wouldn't register on the scale of childhood trauma.

"The sad truth is that children across the ages have suffered horrific trauma of untold proportion and thus have borne a veritable cross of iron from that trauma throughout their lives.

"My comfortable childhood of class privilege wanted for nothing and never knew trauma. My childhood slights are but the shadow of a cross, yet I bear them as the weight of an iron cross. So why can't I let them go?"

"First," Lynette remarked, "believe and accept your experiences and perceptions of your family relationships growing up. Your memories are as valid as those of anyone in your family. But your family's reaction to your story is not surprising."

She explained that family members commonly deny, deflect, and dismiss the truth when a sibling exposes family secrets or attempts to make sense of complicated family relationships.

"Your siblings may never be ready to explore the dynamics of your family and how it affected each of you," she added.

With thoughtful eyes, Lynette studied me for a moment, then spoke words I'd never heard.

"Marise, you suffered a traumatic childhood," she stated. I leaned in with rapt curiosity.

"The cumulative micro-dismissals and sideswipes, the expressions of disgust, and the voices of disdain are no less corrosive than a single, major trauma.

"Your trauma is not what happened to you but what failed to happen.

"Every child has a fundamental need to feel seen, known, and loved for who she is," she remarked.

"But your feelings were ignored, your presence devalued, and your sensitivity invalidated.

"Implicit was the message that you don't matter, so you learned to hide your expression of who you are so as not to bother your family. But doing so emotionally restrains you from being who you are meant to be.

"The invisible experience of what failed to happen," she said, "along with the shaming environment of your childhood and the countless voices of others implicitly chanting the narrative that you're not enough, sculpted your belief that you are flawed and insignificant, thereby unworthy of love and connection."

She added that we carry those beliefs about ourselves into our adult relationships because we humans are drawn into relationships that mirror the relationship patterns we learned as children. I returned a puzzled look.

"I would guess, Marise, that you feel unseen, unknown, unloved, and not accepted as your authentic self in your marriage and that you hide your expression of who you are so as not to burden your spouse."

Moved to tears, I nodded in silent agreement at her perception of my marriage.

I glanced at my watch; it was nearly seven p.m. We gathered our things and headed for the parking lot.

"You seem to have unusual insight into family dynamics and self-understanding," I said. "Do you have some experience with that?"

Lynette smiled sweetly. "I'm a licensed clinical therapist," she replied.

"I was in practice for five years, but then I took time off until my children started school. I'm returning to practice next week; today is my last day volunteering at the nursing home."

"How wonderful!" I exclaimed, clutching her hand in mine. "Thank you for your friendship. I especially appreciate your gift of presence. I yearned to be understood and affirmed. Thank you for holding space for me."

"That's what spiritual directors do best," she remarked, smiling as she started her sedan to depart. "You see, I'm also a certified spiritual director. So, I hold space for whomever God assigns me."

I watched the sedan taillights disappear around the corner and then gazed skyward at the salmon-pink light of the warm spring evening, awestruck by what transpired that day.

After seeking mental health therapy, spiritual direction, and self-direction, I finally surrendered my broken oars and rusty sextant in utter dependence on God.

Then, by his design, God supplanted my need with the gift of presence from an unexpected friendship with a pastor's wife, who was no less a therapist and a spiritual director.

I never saw Lynette after that. But the space Lynette held for me that day eased the cross of the emotional poverty of my childhood.

The Bequest

Two months later, the last weekend of May found me at a Jesuit retreat house in St. Louis.

A "silent" retreat whereby retreatants remain silent throughout four days of reflection, prayer, and Mass, it was the perfect weekend getaway for an avowed introvert like me.

After sharing my "Bread of Life" story, I sought the retreat for healing and release from my siblings' ostracizing shame.

In four months since sharing my story, I had yet to summon the courage to reach out to them or to write my next journal entry, so great was my anguish.

But a chance encounter with a priest that weekend set forth an unexpected circumstance that would loosen the fetters of my shame six weeks later.

I saw Fr. Lawrence one day at the retreat for the Sacrament of Reconciliation, during which I shared that I have teenage twin sons. Before absolution, he ordered a penance of two Hail Marys, but with special instructions:

"Instead of praying '…Holy Mary, Mother of God, pray for *us sinners now and at the hour of our death*,' substitute your sons' names for '*us sinners*' so that you pray for them."

"Thank you, Father, I will do so," I replied.

I then retired to the Chapel to pray my penance but felt a bit unsettled at the priest's instruction, fearing it might be a macabre foretelling of the death of either or both sons.

Indeed, the chilling thought of losing my children shadowed me for days. So, while in the Adoration Chapel the following week, I contemplated my former coworker, Randall, and his wife, Kathryn, who have lost two sons.

Their eldest died years ago in a car accident at age fifteen. Then, only a year ago, their youngest, Liam, who was twenty-four, died in a car wreck.

I learned of their youngest son's death when I saw the couple, who belong to a different parish, the year before at the groundbreaking ceremony of the new Jesus Sun of Justice Church.

Numb with grief, they shared that Liam had died in an automobile accident three days earlier. I couldn't fathom their heartbreak.

Upon learning of their son's death, I considered sending a card. But a card would be a token of solace for the devastating loss. So, I did nothing.

Now, a year after Liam's death, I couldn't imagine how Randall and Katheryn were coping. Yet, what could I offer as a salve to their loss?

So, while in the Adoration Chapel later that day, I sought inspiration from The Little Flower.

"Marise, my friend, pen a poem with words from your heart and give them a white rose bush to remember their son," St. Thérèse intimated.

A rose bush? What a novel idea! But compose a poem? I hesitated – I hadn't written poetry since high school.

I discovered the joy of writing poetry in Mr. Locherbie's Honors English class at Victory Prep. Then, after graduating from Victory Prep, I devoted my summer free time to writing poetry.

In my hardback journal, I practiced penning verses of all genres and forms: limericks and haikus, sonnets and ballads, metered and free-form, concrete and abstract, absurd and profound, inspirational and controversial.

Early one morning, before I left for college, my mother spotted me writing poetry on the patio.

"Writing poetry ... again?" she questioned.

"Umm... yeah..." I replied with an apologetic tone.

"I suppose you'll bring a long-haired kook home from college and tell me, 'But Mom, he writes beautiful poetry,'" she remarked, her voice dripping with mockery.

With head down and eyes averted, I spoke not a word but made my way to my room, where I flung my journal into a nondescript storage box.

Mom's right, I recollected thinking. Writing poetry is kooky, and I should thank her for saving me the shame of my oddball poetry.

Unfortunately, I never retrieved my poetry journal, which found its fate in the landfill months later.

In fact, in thirty years since that summer morning, I composed only two pieces of poetry – each upon the death of my mother and then my father.

A decade earlier, I penned a poem in remembrance of my mother, which was read at her funeral.

Then, when my father died four years later, I wrote in celebration of his life a set of five limericks, which, too, were read at his funeral.

In the Adoration Chapel that day, I pondered what I would write in poetic form that wouldn't sound trite for the grieving couple.

"Marise, offer your poetry to God, and he will imbue your craft with words of hope for Randall and Kathryn," I intuited my patron saint advising me.

"And with your poem, give them a bush abloom with roses white, tied with green, white, and gold ribbons."

Of course! I exclaimed to myself. Those were the colors of Liam's high school.

The next day, I dropped into the local garden store, where I purchased a tall, healthy rosebush with a cluster of white buds on the cusp of bloom.

Unfortunately, time did not allow for procrastination—my saint requested I give them a rose bush with blooms. So, I vowed to compose the poem to deliver the rose-clad shrub to Randall's workplace on Monday morning.

I attended early Mass that Sunday, where I prayed for inspiration, for I was at a loss for words to compose my poem.

I finally settled at my writing desk that afternoon to pen the poem. Two hours later, with the poem nearly complete, I sat dumbfounded at composing the last stanza.

So, I thus asked God to inscribe upon my soul the words he needed me to write, after which the Holy Spirit revealed the more profound meaning of the colored ribbons.

Within minutes I composed the final stanza, along with a brief note to Randall and Kathryn explaining my gift:

Dear Randall and Kathryn,

This is Marise Gallica, your former coworker. I'm writing to let you know I'm thinking of you.

It's hard to believe it's been a year since Liam died. So, I'm reaching out to you as I understand that the anniversary date of losing a loved one can be a day of grieving.

I offer this gift of a rose bush in memory of Liam. Although I didn't have the pleasure of knowing Liam, I could tell from his obituary and the comments that he was a compassionate and beloved son.

My patron saint, St. Thérèse de Lisieux, "The Little Flower," inspired me to send you a message of love in the form of a rose bush and a poem, which I composed especially for you, Randall, and Kathryn.

Please know that I keep you and your family in my prayers.

Marise Gallica

At the Bequest of St. Thérèse, The Little Flower
One day not long ago, I sat in quiet contemplation
In a solemn, sacred space in the Chapel of Adoration.
I gazed through stately windows at a sky of brilliant blue.
It called to mind the month of June, and then I thought of you.

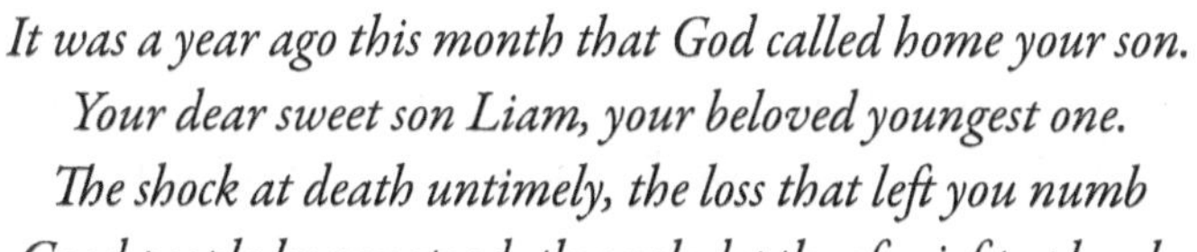

It was a year ago this month that God called home your son.
Your dear sweet son Liam, your beloved youngest one.
The shock at death untimely, the loss that left you numb
Good people by you stood, through depths of grief to plumb.

I couldn't help but think, as the weeks and months sped past,
Their lives returned to normal, while your life in grief was cast.
In prayer, I did thus ask St. Thérèse, The Little Flower.
How might I send a bit of hope and love upon you shower.

Then to my soul, the saint thus spoke: Send roses linen white,
No mere long-stem single bud, but a bush abloom with petals bright.
The complexion of innocence, the luminosity of perfection,
For the soul of their beloved son, white mirrors a splendid spiritual reflec-
tion.

And when the snowy blooms burst forth, she said, may it be easier to cope,
Each bud is God's expression of love, tinctured with the fragrance of hope.
And so, may the roses bloom abundantly, may hope blossom in their
hearts.
And may peace be theirs in knowing, Liam's gentle spirit never parts.

The Little Flower then bade me adorn the shrub with ribbons three:
A sash of white to remember, God embraces Liam for eternity
A strand of gold to honor, Liam's compassionate way of giving.
And a ribbon of green for hope, through God and loving and living.
Marise Gallica

The following day, I left the ribbon-tied rose bush with the poem at the reception desk at Randall's workplace and then headed to my job on the other side of the city.

Yet within minutes, the warmth of giving the novel gift and heartfelt poem grew cold; I could only conclude that I overstepped the inviolable boundary of the couple's grief.

"Oh, dear! What have I done?" I uttered aloud to myself. "Liam died a year ago, and Randall and Kathryn do not want to be reminded of their son's death."

I could only believe that grief has an uncanny way of reseeding itself, and the couple would not appreciate a gift that re-awakens their grief. Hence, I chided myself for being impulsive and inconsiderate.

Moreover, suppose the couple perceives my poem as syrupy and superficial, I conjectured with self-condemnation.

For the next four weeks, I anxiously checked my text messages, email, and postal mail for the couple's response. Alas! None was forthcoming.

With each crestfallen instance, I intuited the gentle voice of St. Thérèse, enjoining me to have faith and trust in God, but to no avail.

Clutched by shame over my poem, I begged God to grant me the grace of detachment from the couple's acknowledgment of my gift.

Four weeks later, I settled into a pew six rows from the back for the weekday noon Mass at the Cathedral of Mary, Queen of Angels.

A practice I began during Lent, I attended noon Mass at the grand cathedral twice a week as my schedule allowed.

As Mass commenced, a handsome couple slipped into a pew across the aisle and one row up from where I sat. My heart lurched—it was Randall and Kathryn!

In four months of random attendance at noon Mass, I'd never spotted the couple there. Nonetheless, we met eyes upon returning to our pews after Communion, and then after Mass, we could do nothing but greet with warm hugs and slight tears.

"I left you a voicemail after receiving your gift," Randall said. "We built a new home recently, and we called to thank you and invite you to our housewarming party."

"Oh, dear! I hadn't thought to check my voicemail," I whispered sheepishly.

"We were deeply moved at receiving the rose bush and the meaning of your beautiful poem," Kathryn assured me. "St. Thérèse is my patron saint, too, and the rose bush holds special significance for me. I've planted the rosebush in my garden at our new home, and it is growing beautifully!"

We departed the church together and then bid cordial goodbyes.

I stood astonished at the synchronicity. I prayed for release from shame at my writing, and God heard my plea!

Indeed, Divine Providence led me and the couple to the sacred space of an unplanned weekday Mass in an unlikely church and thereby delivered to each the rich grace of in-person connection—a blessing unmatched by text message, email, phone call, or postal mail.

That night in the Adoration Chapel, I reflected on the life-affirming grace of authentic connection God granted me through Randall and Kathryn's presence in person after Mass.

No doubt, the couple's warm hugs and kind words affirmed that they received my poem as beautifully written, personally moving, and spiritually meaningful.

Then the Holy Spirit revealed the Divine orchestration of that day's astounding synchronicity:

I sought healing from the shame of my writing, and Divine Providence thus placed an unusual penance from an unfamiliar priest before me.

The penance called to mind Randall and Kathryn's loss, after which St. Thérèse requested I pen a poem for the grieving parents. Thus, I answered God's call to share my gift, and God poured forth his blessing in return.

Awash in the warm, Divine Presence of the Blessed Sacrament, I bowed my head and offered profound gratitude for the gift of writing, a worthy expression of my authentic self, for which I am no longer ashamed.

"I will embrace your gift, God, and write what you call me to," I prayed, "I now understand that you are at work in me, and with me, and through me."

Lo! Therein my prayer, I envisioned the presence of The Little Flower, her hands clasped in reverent delight against her Carmel habit and her radiant presence beaming upon me amidst the splendor of a million white petals of Divine love.

God is good!

To: Marise Gallica

From: Theodore Locherbie

Subject: Remarks – "The Metanoia"

Marise,

I have finished reviewing "The Metanoia," and I am awestruck by the riveting, emotive quality of your writing and the introspective depth of your story.

You capture with deft writing the various twists and turns and rejections and sensitivities that have surfaced from your siblings' reactions to your seeking clarity, understanding, and truth of how your childhood experiences have impacted you throughout your life!

Your writing is piercing, probing, parallel, and revelatory!

Countless readers will identify with the pain that, as a child and later as an adult "child," they feel seen only when they fall short and cherished only if they don't stir others' vulnerability.

The title of your story is profoundly meaningful and telling, as "metanoia" means a transformative change of heart, especially of a spiritual conversion, which fits beautifully with the collection of narratives you have developed thus far.

Moreover, I found incredibly profound your insight into how one's sense of shame and inadequacies can keep him from feeling worthy of God's love and relationship!

The removal of Moses' sandals so that he could approach God in His holiness works exceptionally well with your own needs to "untie" your own "sandal," or rather, the false identity of shame that others assigned to you.

As your writing mentor, I can appreciate the emotive quality of your writing and the depth of meaning in your story.

Nonetheless, I am concerned with your dilemmas: how to avoid rejection and anger from your siblings if you tell "your story." But you need to make peace with your past to find joy, purpose, and self-love.

Regards, Theodore Locherbie

To: Theodore Locherbie

From: Marise Gallica

Subject: Remarks–"The Metanoia"

Mr. Locherbie,

Thank you for your candid remarks. No doubt, I've contemplated how I might tell this story without endangering my tenuous sibling ties and denigrating my family's dignity.

My spouse and siblings' antipathy of my writing devastated me for months. No doubt, as portrayed in this chapter, their shaming reinforced my shame identity and disintegrated my passion for writing.

Paralyzed by shame, I could neither suspend nor move forward on my book project. To halt the project would be to retreat into "hiding" and thus allow my false identity of shame to reign victorious.

Yet, to proceed with the truth would be to forego any hope of reconciliation with my siblings.

But, alas! Therein festered the painful irony of my narrative—a loop of shame from which only God could set me free. Yet, my encounter with Randall and Kathryn at Mass was the movement of the Holy Spirit through which God liberated me from that shame.

Regards, Marise

Chapter 9 The Hummingbird

To: Theodore Locherbie

From: Marise Gallica

Subject: "The Hummingbird"

Mr. Locherbie,

This narrative, "The Hummingbird," centers around my praying the Rosary.

A Catholic devotional, the Rosary is composed of five decades of Hail Marys, each representing a momentous event in the life of Jesus or Mary. Each decade invites meditation upon the spiritual meaning of the event.

Catholics believe that when prayed with intention and focus, the Rosary can make the devotee more receptive to the spiritual fruit of each meditation, such as humility, patience, perseverance, obedience, love of neighbor, joy in Jesus, finding Jesus through Mary, and other graces.

Hence, I share with you "The Hummingbird," a narrative describing astonishing synchronicity and, more so, an invaluable spiritual revelation.

Regards, Marise

Dear St. Thérèse,

I share with you today my narrative of breathtaking synchronicity that I can only describe as a message of Divine Truth, delivered to me with haste through the Blessed Virgin Mary, the Mediatrix of all Graces.

In friendship, Marise

The Hummingbird

I attended early Mass at Jesus Sun of Justice Church on the last Sunday of July. Then, after Mass, I found a seat at the monthly Reflections of Justice Committee meeting held that morning in the church office.

During the meeting, the group discussed expanding its dissent of the government's ill-treatment of migrants through a letter-writing campaign to Congressional senators and representatives.

I sat quietly throughout the discussion, for I had nothing new to contribute. But near the end of the meeting, something moved me to speak.

"We could pray about it," I blurted from my side of the table.

All fell silent as if startled at the suggestion.

"I mean... um ... we should absolutely keep writing letters," I declared emphatically, "but we could pray about it, too!"

My proposal met with palpable resistance expressed from around the table:

"We can't just sit around and pray about it...."

"Praying about it won't affect the changes that must be made...."

"We have to take action...."

"We must act now, not just pray...."

"Action is prayer...."

"Prayer through action gives the best results...."

Those who refrained from comment either crossed their arms in nonverbal defense or looked down or away to feign disengagement.

Finally, recognizing no ally around the table, I stayed seated but mentally retreated from the discussion as the meeting meandered toward adjournment.

I departed the meeting feeling a bit unsettled. So, later that afternoon, I sought comfort in the solitude of my peaceful backyard and the joy of the sun-spangled summer day.

I settled into my porch glider to pray the Rosary, a daily ritual I incorporated into my prayer life weeks prior, and then silently recounted the meeting.

Around the table that morning sat the laity of the Jesus Sun of Justice Church ministries: sacristans and Eucharistic ministers, lectors and choir members, political activists and social justice advocates, and a handful of devotees to Holy Day and weekday Mass.

Good and well-meaning people they are, I mused. So I should feel safe proposing prayer with the Reflections of Justice Committee.

Instead, the group's overt resistance to prayer as integral to social justice action felt more like that of a secular, political action committee versus a faith-centered lay ministry.

"I felt scorned and invalidated at today's meeting, and I didn't know what to do," I confided in prayer to Mary, Mediatrix of All Graces.

I then elected to pray the Luminous Mysteries of the Rosary, whose fourth decade is the Mystery of the Transfiguration, which yields the fruit of spiritual courage.

I closed my eyes and began to pray.

Then, typical of my prayer practice, within the first decade of the silent utterance of the mantra-like Hail Mary, I assumed a light meditative state whereby the mind tunes out irrelevant surrounding noise.

But upon starting the fourth decade, I detected a faint timbre of unknown origin emanating from the hibiscus bush near the porch.

I opened my eyes and peered at the shrub, an imposing, sturdy perennial laden with saucer-size blooms in heavenly hues of creamy white and peppermint pink.

Lo! Upon a white bloom hovered a hummingbird with a meadowlark yellow breast and earthy brown wings.

I paused my Rosary recitation and gazed awestruck at the confection of bird aflutter before me, for in twenty-five years in my home, I'd never spotted a hummingbird in my yard.

The bird flitted aloft and then alighted upon a utility line above. We caught each other's eye and studied the other for a moment.

But then, the precious bird took flight and fluttered away, swooping and looping and then disappearing over the wooden back fence.

I couldn't help but ponder the meaning of the bird's unexpected presence.

I last saw a hummingbird thirty years ago when my mother affectionately pointed to a handsome red hummingbird hovering about the colorful flowers outside her kitchen window.

Indeed, as I was growing up and until she died, my mother believed in a deep spiritual connection with the red hummingbird.

She oft' declared with conviction that the bird, a rare sighting in her garden, was a visible sign of God's presence, for it appeared only in her times of great spiritual need.

The recollection of my mother's spiritual connection with the bird called forth memories of my mother as a state legislator thirty years ago. I benignly forgot about my Rosary in progress as I reflected on her vocation as a public servant.

Throughout her twelve years as a legislator, my mother courageously faced staunch death penalty proponents and partisan politics by opposing the death penalty on the legislature floor.

Throughout her three terms, her fearless advocacy for pro-life legislation for imprisoned persons was instrumental in defeating countless death-penalty bills.

She often remarked that her days in the legislature were difficult, especially when tackling divisive issues such as the death penalty.

She sought spiritual nourishment through daily Mass and weekly Adoration throughout her twelve years as a legislator.

I visited the Statehouse once in my early twenties, watching her oppose a death penalty bill.

The last lawmaker to take the floor before the final vote, my mother, the legislator, spoke with untold conviction against the bill.

Her words spellbound her colleagues on both sides of the aisle and a packed gallery of media, death penalty proponents, and opponents.

A narrow vote that day defeated the bill that year.

I called my mother later that night, commending her speech and inquiring how long she rehearsed it, for she spoke without notes or a written speech.

"How did you know what to speak, and how did you speak with such conviction?" I queried.

"I don't remember what I said on the floor today, Marise," my mother remarked. "I only knew I'd done my homework and taken the office politicking as far as possible.

"I prepared no speech," she continued. "When I took the floor, I could do nothing but entrust my words to the Holy Spirit.

"Without the Holy Spirit, my words would be nothing but clanging cymbals," she added in a fading voice. (Note that it would be years before I realized that "clanging cymbals" was referenced in St. Paul's Letter to the Corinthians, 13:1).

I waited for my mother to continue, for she suddenly fell silent.

"You see, Marise," my mother whispered in a voice choked with emotion, "Of such poverty of spirit am I that I can do nothing without God."

I recalled rolling my eyes at my mother waxing religious again. I was a young adult with a long-contentious relationship with my mother and a cradle Catholic en route to becoming a disaffected Catholic. Her words were lost on me that night.

I gazed at the white bloom where the hummingbird made known its presence only moments before, drawing forth the memory of my mother's words that night three decades ago: "Of such poverty of spirit am I that I can do nothing without God."

Then, my soul clutched at the meaning of her words and emotions and the truth of spiritual courage.

The truth struck me that only through humility and complete dependence on God in all things could my mother receive the grace of spiritual courage for her vocation as a public servant.

Likewise, through the poverty of Spirit and complete dependence on God, I, too, could receive the grace of spiritual courage.

I marveled at the synchronicity reflected in the unanticipated presence of the beautiful bird:

I prayed the Rosary, seeking the grace of spiritual courage, at which Mary, the Mediatrix of All Grace, hastened to enlighten me. For as I prayed the fourth decade–the Mystery of the Transfiguration, which invites meditation on the grace of spiritual courage–Mary illuminated the truth of that grace through the rare presence of a hummingbird. This spirit creature symbolizes my mother's connection to God.

Without God, I can do nothing lest my words are but clanging cymbals. So, too, neither can any individual, group, or congregation proceed toward well-intended action without God, lest its voice is a clanging cymbal.

Then, enfolded in the joy of Divine Truth, I thus prayed the final decades of the Rosary in the peaceful solitude of my summer garden.

To: Marise Gallica

    From: Theodore Locherbie

    Subject: Remarks-"The Hummingbird"

    Marise,

This interconnected story and experience, which revealed the importance and power of the Holy Spirit, is my favorite story yet of the narratives you've developed so far!

You make a great connection concerning the need to have prayer as an integral part of moral action. Indeed, I like how you brought out the hypocritical weakness of religious bodies who fail to use and prioritize prayer in their decisions and action.

Moreover, the rare appearance of the hummingbird and its connection to your mother's spiritual insights provide an uplifting tone concerning your relationship with your mom.

This story highlights your deft description of details, such as those surrounding the hibiscus bush, which is one of the greatest strengths of your writing style.

Regards, Theodore Locherbie

Chapter 10 The Prelude

To: Theodore Locherbie

    From: Marise Gallica

    Subject: "The Prelude"

    Mr. Locherbie,

    I have emailed you another chapter, "The Prelude." But after I sent it, I realized that Victory Prep Academy is moving classes online in response to the COVID-19 pandemic.

    So, I suspect that you're preparing materials for the fourth nine weeks. But I'm in no rush. Given the anticipated demands on nurses with the pandemic surge, I am uncertain when I can resume work on my book.

    I originally intended "The Prelude" to be a short section of my concluding chapter. But once I unearth the gem of a story, I discover the treasure of more gems within it.

    As always, I eagerly await your commentary and feedback.

    Regards, Marise

Dear St. Thérèse,

I'm thrilled to share that after decades of being silenced by the voice of self-condemnation, I shared the gift of my music today, playing piano for an audience for the first time in forty-five years. My story, "The Prelude," portrays the sweet Providence that led me to that moment.

More so, my narrative describes my joy of discovering that part of my authentic self that, for years, stayed muted by my false identity of shame.

In friendship, Marise

The Prelude

The Invitation

My unexpected encounter with Randall and Kathryn at weekday Mass overwhelmed me with joy for weeks. No doubt, the energy of that astounding instance of sacred presence, orchestrated by Divine Providence, melted the shame that for months held frozen my motivation to write.

As summer yielded to autumn, I began composing "The Metanoia." This narrative, I hoped, would offer the gift of presence to others who discover within themselves a false identity of shame.

Moreover, I presumed the chapter's ending – my calling to embrace God's gift of writing – marked the inspiring, natural conclusion to this leg of my journey.

But God was planning the prelude to my next chapter, which commenced on a sparkling autumn day.

Weeks after my chance encounter with Randall and Kathryn, the activities director of the nursing home in the north wing of the hospital popped into my office.

"I heard you like to play the piano!" she announced.

I shot her a deer-in-the-headlights look.

"We're having a talent show in October, and we'd like you to play," she proclaimed.

"Umm... I do play, but not in front of people," I stammered. "I'll be opting out but thank you for the invitation."

"No worries, there's plenty of time if you change your mind," she chirped, darting out the door.

In that instant, my mind flashed back to a chapel on a humid spring morning in April 1979, where, being the next contestant in the district middle school piano contest, I sat with the other ninth-grade contestants waiting to perform.

I'll be fine; I've played my piece by memory for weeks, I reassured myself as I settled onto the piano bench, which faced away from the audience. I poised my hands over the keyboard, ready to begin.

But, alas! The penetrating eyes of the other contestants overwhelmed me, and the entire piece escaped my memory!

In a flummoxed panic, I tried to jog my memory of the opening notes, but to no avail.

The prolonged pause of anticipation pierced the air with uncomfortable silence.

Finally, with cheeks burning, I arose from the bench and, in surreal numbness, made my way to the adjudicator's table at the back of the room, where I scanned the first few measures of the piece to boost my recall.

I returned to the piano and commenced my piece, a Beethoven sonatina composed of three movements traversing six pages.

But alas! Enfeebled by the anxiety of judgment by peers, my performance faltered. Indeed, like the classic failed performance of a figure skater, my minor memory lapse ignited a chain reaction of trips and falls at every turn of the piece until the final pitiful chord.

I skulked back to my seat and sunk back into my chair. Around me sat four classmates, who each performed with enviable technique and exquisite interpretation.

Naturally gifted with smarts, looks, talent, and poise, they comprised the elite cadre of our ninth-grade class.

"You lack talent and skill, and you'll never have the mettle to play for an audience," rasped my voice of self-condemnation.

Believing that no greater shipwreck had a piano solo been seen, I thus, on that April morning, secretly determined never to risk shame for playing where others might hear.

I never mentioned it to her because I was ashamed of my performance and feared further shaming from my mother. Moreover, I could only recall that my mother neither bid me good luck on my solo that morning nor queried how it went that night.

For years I could only conclude that her lack of inquiry signified that I didn't matter.

Neither did I debrief details of my tattered performance with my music teacher, Ms. Bachelder, who, when I mentioned that my solo hit rough spots, dismissed my assessment and then turned to my next assignment.

Because of my busy schedule, I took a break from lessons that summer. But secretly, I knew I would never resume them. In fact, I stopped playing piano altogether.

No one seemed to notice.

The Theme

I sat back in my office chair, pondering the invitation to play for my coworkers and the theme of pianos throughout my life.

I played my first recital at age six when, as a first grader at St. Augustine Grade School, I joined my siblings in a Christmas Eve recital at our teacher's home, our Aunt Carolyn. Our aunt lived two blocks from St. Augustine's Church, and the pastor joined us that night for the early evening family gathering.

With nary a self-conscious regard, I eagerly played the classic carol, "Oh Come, Little Children," on the blonde upright piano in Aunt Carolyn's living room, at which all politely applauded.

Exuberant with joy, I couldn't wait for my next recital!

I continued lessons with various teachers throughout grade school, which saw daily practice on the old baby grand in the living room of my childhood home.

I usually practiced before supper, learning to tune out clatter and chatter from the nearby kitchen as dinner was prepared.

I frequently played after helping with the dinner dishes, too. I often heard my father sink into his armchair in the corner behind me to peruse medical journals while I practiced.

Of course, my father never opined about my playing, and I never sought his opinion. But from an early age, I believed his regular, silent presence affirmed my authentic joy of playing the piano.

My last teacher, Ms. Bachelder, taught lessons in her home, where under her kind tutelage, I sat at her black baby grand piano each week as a middle school student, further refining my piano skills.

Ironically, as a first-time homeowner two decades later, I purchased Ms. Bachelder's residence, where for twenty-five years, I've made my home in the 1950s ranch-style house with curved walk and filigree front porch pillars.

A permanent bookshelf now resides where her baby grand piano once sat. My old battered upright piano sits on the other side of the room, where sadly, I left it untouched for years.

Despite years of lessons, I played only one recital after my Christmas Eve debut at age six. Nonetheless, I performed my seventh- and eighth-grade contest solos without distress, so why did I clutch in my ninth-grade contest? I pondered.

Then, the falsehood to which I clung for forty years became evident. I lacked neither talent, skill, nor mettle. Instead, I clutched because my practice environment changed that year!

A sibling won a new upright piano in a workplace contest the previous summer. Unsuitable for her studio apartment, the piano was placed in my room.

Indeed, the piano presence in my room invited frequent and focused practice, and my skills advanced appreciably that school year.

But the situation proved unfavorable for the musicianship of an introvert prone to social anxiety. Sequestered in my room at the back of the house, I no longer practiced in my father's and family's indirect audience.

No wonder I clutched that morning in 1979, I exclaimed to myself. I was merely unaccustomed to playing for an audience.

The Affirmation

For decades I stayed frozen in the identity of a pianist unworthy of performance. But that identity began to thaw on a brisk winter evening two years ago while in the Adoration Chapel at the Cana Retreat Center.

As I meditated that night, the quiet chapel air carried to my ears the muffled tones of piano music emanating from the celebration of Mass in the adjacent chapel, the Chapel of Mary the First Disciple.

The main chapel in the monastery-like retreat center, the Chapel of Mary, comprises a sacred space of noble simplicity whose only artwork is a breathtaking mural depicting "The Annunciation."

The mural gracing the chapel wall portrays in delicate relief the moment when the Angel Gabriel announced to Mary that God chose her to be the mother of Jesus.

Throughout weeks of daily Adoration, I'd yet to hear the chapel piano played. But so entranced was I by the sweet music that I stayed to listen until Mass concluded.

More so, I was absorbed in the long-lost recollection of the joy of playing piano in my childhood.

After Mass, I peeked into the empty chapel and then caught my breath when I spied the maple-brown baby grand piano nestled in the corner in the back.

With a surge of exuberance unknown for years, I departed the Cana Retreat Center that night, vowing to play the chapel's baby grand piano as soon as possible.

A drab Sunday evening one month later found me at the Retreat Center, where I saw not a soul upon entering the unlocked building.

I made my way to the Chapel of Mary and placed a yellowing, dog-eared music book upon the piano's music rack, its front cover long lost.

The last book I played before abandoning piano in adolescence, the book included "Prelude in C Major" by J.S. Bach. The song, commonly recognized as a famous rendition of "Ave Maria," stands as my favorite hymn since childhood.

I sat silently on the bench, preparing to play the piece I hadn't played for decades. I inhaled a deep breath and then, with tentative fingers, began to play.

With chime-like quality, the simple, elegant melody graced the sacred hush of the chapel. Thus, I marveled at the pure joy of playing the piano for the first time in decades.

I played the piece again, and the chapel door creaked open behind me. I paused and glanced over my shoulder to spot the receptionist, whom I didn't know personally, peering at me through the cracked door.

"You play so beautifully," she remarked. "Don't let me stop you," she implored, closing the door gently behind her.

Buoyed by the unexpected affirmation that night, I resumed piano lessons that week, and after forty years, I began practicing lessons daily at home.

For months I played classic hymns almost nightly in the intimacy of the Chapel of Mary the First Disciple.

Then, ensconced in the nonjudgmental presence of none other than God, my inhibition at playing the piano began to thaw.

A Friday afternoon in early March found me at the chapel piano, overwhelmed with gratitude. Earlier that day, I received an offer for a new job as a nurse leader, a veritable answer to a desperate prayer!

To celebrate, I played a joyful rendition of "Ave Maria," during which a bicep-thick teenage boy slipped through the door behind me.

From the green and gold track-and-field t-shirt he wore, I presumed he was a student-athlete with a local Catholic high school that held a retreat at the Center that day.

"May I sit and pray while you play?" he inquired in a hushed tone.

"Absolutely," I whispered.

He knelt in prayer in a pew nearby while I continued to play from my hymnal collection. Then, about twenty minutes later, the boy arose to depart.

With eyes brimming with tears and a reverent fist crossing his heart, he bowed and whispered, "Thank you, that was beautiful."

I returned to the chapel to play the following day and again after Mass at Jesus Sun of Justice that Sunday, Laetare Sunday.

Each day as I played, a half-dozen weekend retreatants wandered into the chapel to journal, pray, and meditate. Upon departing, each nodded and smiled in appreciation of my music.

Thus, with each gesture of affirmation, I offered profound gratitude to God for the gift of nonjudgmental acceptance.

The Birthday Gift

My frequent playing in the chapel might've continued indefinitely were it not for God's providential answer to another prayer later that spring.

So enthralled was I at playing the chapel's piano that I yearned for a baby grand in my home. Unable to afford one, I one day casually asked God if he might find me one.

Then, one Sunday in early June, Fr. Pepe announced before Mass that the piano in the sanctuary would need a temporary home while the new church was being built. From my pew, six rows from the back, I instantly envisioned playing the ebony baby grand piano in the living room of my home.

So, I contacted Fr. Pepe with an offer to help and learned that the baby grand in the choir room also needed a temporary home.

"Which piano would you like to store?" Fr. Pepe queried.

Unable to decide, I offered to house both. So, the following Monday, the pianos were delivered to my home. Naturally, I was thrilled, for that day was my birthday!

Indeed, my birthday that year welcomed God's lavish gift to a simple prayer: the delivery of not one—but two—baby grand pianos to my home, whereby I would play them at will for the next eighteen months!

Then, that night, celebrating my birthday, I played on the church's piano hymns of exaltation at God's perfect timing of his birthday gift.

I had only months to play the church's pianos.

Yet to forego the talent show invitation was to decline God's invitation to overcome my shame at playing for others – an invitation made evident by the gift of the church's pianos in my home. Thus, with only two months to practice, I nonetheless accepted the invitation.

The Recital

With my teacher's guidance, I prepared a lovely piece, "L'Hirondelle (The Swallow)," by Frederich Burgmüller. A delightful melody, the song, when played with artistic interpretation, portrays the heavenly flutter of a swallow swooping in graceful arcs through sunbeams and shadows in an old wooden barn.

Emboldened by the weeks of preparation, I awakened the day of the show confident at playing before the non-threatening crowd.

But while preparing for work that morning, a movement of the Holy Spirit inspired me to play a more meaningful selection.

That afternoon about fifty coworkers and patients gathered for the show around the baby grand piano gracing the hospital's elegant cathedral ceiling lobby. When my name was called, I settled upon the bench with hands poised over the keyboard. And then – with nary a notion of self-conscious regard – I delivered a near-perfect performance of "Prelude in C Major" ("Ave Maria").

Amidst a round of warm applause, I arose from the piano. I took a slight bow, offering silent praise and gratitude for the grace of self-compassion and the grace of self-acceptance, which God lavished upon me through his lavish gift of the church's pianos.

The Holy Spirit moved me to play the song that first led me back to my authentic joy of playing the piano. Thus, on a sparkling autumn day, I played my music for none but God, through which he revealed his work to dismantle my false identity of shame.

God is good!

To: Marise Gallica

From: Theodore Locherbie

Subject: The Prelude

Marise,

I have finished reviewing your narrative, "The Prelude," and I am amazed at your story's incredible interconnections and Godly interventions! See my remarks below:

- Your use of the word "prelude" at the start of your story intrigues me, for it ties nicely to your chapter title and the title of your recital solo! Although I didn't recognize this connection in my first reading.

- What an insightful interconnection you make between your mother's acknowledgment of your piano solo and your lifelong internalization of this being another instance of feeling unimportant in your mother's eyes.

• Your interconnection between buying the home of your former piano teacher and then revealing your piano's placement in your home offers a nuanced revelation of how you distanced yourself from your earlier painful experience at the piano for decades.

• Your later connection of playing in the chapel from the book you last played signifies an invitation from your authentic self to revisit—and thus make whole—the truth of the genuine joy of playing the piano.

• Moreover, your inclusion of three examples of others affirming your musical prowess speaks to the blessings you describe.

• In the Birthday Gift section, what a spectacular God-intervention and God-blessing of two grand pianos, not just one.

• Likewise, eighteen months provided the time you needed to restore your musical confidence. So, your preparation for the looming workplace talent show provided an opportunity to gain self-acceptance and joy in playing the piano.

What a magnificent connection of events that go beyond coincidences but fit the realm of God-incidences!

• With The Recital section, your readers will appreciate that your narrative reveals what moved you that morning to play the song that led you back to your joy of playing the piano vs. the music you'd practiced so ardently.

Your receptivity to the movement of the Spirit and the affirmation you received in playing the song provided the needed "healing" touch to your story and experience!

• For your conclusion, may I suggest that you encapsulate how God's myriad interventions helped heal the scars of decades of self-effacement once you petitioned Him in prayer, thus your exclamation that "God is good!"

Overall, I find profoundly moving the unbelievable "God-incidences" you have experienced and thus revealed through this narrative.

Regards, Theodore Locherbie

To: Theodore Locherbie

From: Marise Gallica

Mr. Locherbie,

Thank you for your substantive remarks. Your commentary prompts the following reflection:

• About the "figure skating fail" analogy: I used the word "fail" because, for forty years, that's how my ego informed my understanding of my performance.

In retrospect, though, from the distance of advanced middle age, I finally perceived my middle-school piano performance not with the shame of my musical ineptitude but as a testament to my courage to continue in the moment of overwhelm, despite feeling vulnerable to judgment by my peers.

• The word "lavish" references John 1:3, "See what great love the Father has lavished on us..."

In writing my story, I recognized that God not only blessed me with two pianos. More so, he lavished me with the grace of self-acceptance, self-compassion, and joy, which helped me overcome my false identity as an unworthy pianist.

• My use of the word "falsehood" refers to my ego's long-held belief that I lack musical talent.

• Finally, I appreciate your intriguing insight about the arrangement of my piano teacher's new baby grand compared to my battered upright in my living room and how I "distanced" myself from my early years of playing piano.

Indeed, While composing this narrative, I never considered my furniture arrangement to be a subconscious reflection of my identity. What a perfect, real-life analogy for how I have figuratively distanced myself all these years from my battered sense of self.

As always, thank you for your insightful commentary.
Regards, Marise

Chapter 11 The Rosary

From: Marise Gallica

To: Theodore Locherbie

Subject: "The Rosary"

Mr. Locherbie,

My following narrative describes astonishing synchronicity that might render you speechless.

Regards, Marise

Dear St. Thérèse,

I share with you a narrative that speaks to the grace of reconciliation, healing, hope, and charity, as well as the golden, interwoven threads of synchronicity which led me to receive those graces.

In friendship, Marise

The Rosary

The Grace

Silenced by the voice of self-condemnation for decades, my music that day for the nursing home marked the first time in decades that I played piano for a formal audience.

Yet, that moment arrived not a day too soon. Within weeks, the pianos would be returned in time for the November 22 Consecration Mass for the magnificent new Jesus Sun of Justice Church.

On a pale autumn morning two weeks later, I watched the piano mover's truck pull away from the curb at my home, and then I turned to survey the empty space left by the absent pianos.

For more than a year, the church's pianos kindled the fire of my long-lost joy of playing, I mused. If invited again, I would embrace the chance to play for an audience and consecrate my performance to God again.

Yet my redemption from shame at the piano was a small victory compared to my silent battle for redemption in a relationship with two of my sisters, Marla and Marjorie.

Our connection remained broken a year after their withering rebuke of my "Bread of Life" chapter.

Marla never acknowledged my apology for my story. In fact, in ten months, neither sibling had called, messaged, or visited. Yet neither had I contacted either of them.

So ashamed was I by their chastisement that I could only conclude my siblings' withdrawal of contact confirmed my unworthiness of connection with them.

Although my sister Miriam voiced discomfort with my story, we restored our relationship months later when I shared the story of my unexpected encounter with Randall and Kathryn at Mass. Likewise, my sister Marilyn, who kindly dismissed my "Bread of Life" story, nonetheless voiced no animosity toward me or my story.

Ironically, the glacier of shame from Marjorie and Marla held frozen for months my yearning to finish and publish my story... about shame.

Nonetheless, after my encounter with Randall and Kathryn delivered unanticipated affirmation of my writing, I forged ahead with renewed energy over the next few months, composing the first part of my next chapter, "The Metanoia."

But as summer faded into fall, that energy disintegrated into anguish.

Finishing the chapter would call for recounting my siblings' blistering chastisement in granular detail. Yet so great was my pain that I sought distraction from writing by playing the piano for weeks.

Alas! With the pianos gone, I could no longer defer trying to restore my relationship with my sisters. But, of course, nothing would diminish the cut of my sisters' grievous rebuke except for the balm of reconciliation.

Yet, short of risking raw vulnerability and broaching the matter directly, I was at a loss for how to reconcile. So, despite no longer having the pianos as a distraction, my writing stalled, nonetheless.

The day before Thanksgiving, Miriam called and mentioned that Marjorie, who lives alone, had no plans for Thanksgiving Day. Instead, Marjorie would join Marla and her three college-age children for a Thanksgiving meal later that weekend.

Upon hearing that Marjorie would spend Thanksgiving Day alone, I knew instantly how to reach out to her. So, at mid-morning on Thanksgiving Day, I text-messaged Marjorie in our first communication in nearly a year, inquiring if she was home.

She texted me back within seconds. I promptly responded:

"I have something for you. I'll see you at noon."

Shortly before noon, I appeared at her door laden with an oversized storage bin.

"What's that?" Marjorie queried, holding open the door.

"Wait and see," I exclaimed.

I made my way to the kitchen, where I produced from the bin a table service for two and accouterments of a festive holiday table, complete with my holly berry dinnerware, white linen napkins, and a cheerful holiday centerpiece fresh from the florist.

Upon the table, I set the meal I prepared that morning: a veritable Thanksgiving feast with trimmings—roast duck with gravy, wild rice, sweet potatoes, green beans, corn, beets, dinner rolls, and fresh pumpkin pie homemade from scratch.

As I readied the table, Marjorie stood silently with a hesitant smile and eyes dewy with tears. I prayed grace aloud before we sat down, and then I prayed silently for the grace to regenerate our relationship.

Finally, we commenced the shared feast, whereby in a kitchen bright with afternoon sun, we chatted for hours about our family and friends, our gardens and homes, and our sundry shared interests, interlaced with warmhearted banter.

Throughout our repast, neither she nor I raised the issue of my "Bread of Life" story, for our lifelong familial pattern of conflict denial also found a seat at the table that day.

Yet, as the hours passed, so did our feelings of mutual hurt and vulnerability. Thus, through a feast made rich by the grace of hospitality and kindness, we reset our relationship by sitting at the table and sharing a meal.

I departed Marjorie's home filled with gratitude for the grace bestowed upon our Thanksgiving meal that day. Hence, that night, soothed by the balm of a relationship restored, I set forth with renewed vigor to write my next chapter, "The Metanoia."

The Gall

A pale December afternoon the following week found me sitting across the desk from the director of nursing at a rural nursing home ten miles north of my house.

"When can you start?" she queried, eager to add an experienced nurse to her thin staffing roster.

"I can start in two weeks," I replied as I signed an agreement to work the overnight shift every Friday and Saturday for months into the near future.

I departed the interview thrilled to make extra money but galled by the need to do so. Despite my job at Mercy Senior Care Hospital, where I enjoyed collegial relationships, enviable autonomy, and a corner office with a window, the position paid less than my previous jobs.

So, therein coursed the gall: the breadth of support I hoped to receive from Carl was never forthcoming.

From the vision disability benefits received on behalf of his dependents, Carl gave me only a fraction each month. A paltry sum, the support was a pittance for raising our two strapping teenage boys.

I paused in bittersweet reminiscence, recollecting that upon the birth of our twins, I chose to stay in the relationship. I recalled imagining God blessed us with twins because we were supposed to be together. Perchance ours might unfold into an epic love story, affectionately retold over holiday dinners for generations.

Indeed, Carl and I wed twelve years later. On a golden summer day three years ago, Fr. Pepe blessed our marriage in a small Catholic chapel attended by family and scores of friends.

A lovely reception followed in St. Peter Claver Hall in the former St. Peter Claver Church, the only African American Catholic church in the diocese until its closure fifty years ago.

Yet the superficial trappings of marriage never materialized. Instead, our households, finances, friends, faith, and future remained separate; our lives drifted apart.

Except for our children, the only element we had in common was... we had nothing in common.

Despite the pronounced estrangement, Carl summarily denied my request for divorce, stating, "I won't agree to divorce unless the boys live with me for six months, and you have to pay me child support for half the year!"

Of course, after our teenage boys deemed their father's demand unfeasible, further discussion of divorce halted indefinitely.

I would have to bide time until the boys turned eighteen, when child support was no longer an issue.

Indeed, our three-year marriage occupied the peculiar state of being married yet never married. We were legally married, but the marriage never authentically materialized. We never made a home together, but we could not agree on a divorce. Yet since we never shared assets, neither could we claim legal separation and thus financial reparations either.

Finding no recourse, I had no choice but to take a second job. So, one week later, my indignation at Carl was so great that I began another Twenty-Four Glory Be novena on Sunday.

Seeing no way out of the toxic relationship, I yearned for a sign that God would release me from the marriage.

The next day I mentioned to Carl that I was starting a second job at a nursing home. "Congratulations!" he exclaimed in a booming voice, genuine with ardor.

I cast a sideways scowl. But alas! My dismay was lost on him, for his vision condition renders imperceptible the facial features and gestures of others. Yet, in that instant, Jesus flooded my heart with charity for Carl and the suffering he bears to his vision impairment.

In hopeless silence, I inhaled a deep breath, and then at once, I felt sheepish at the self-serving tenor of my first two days' petition.

In my silence, I finally understood that I needed not a sign that God would release me from a complicated relationship but the grace to bear the relationship until God wills my release. So, with a humble heart, I recanted my earlier petition and petitioned only for grace sufficient for my relationship with Carl for the remainder of my novena.

The Luminous Night

I was to report for my first shift at the nursing home on a Friday, three days after Christmas Day.

Uncertain whether the rigors of night shift nursing might drain my energy for writing, I was determined to finish "The Metanoia" before starting the job.

I finally finished the long-fought chapter on Sunday, two days before Christmas. That evening I took a welcome break to shop for groceries and decorations for my Christmas Day festivities.

As I headed onto the highway for my Christmas errands, I spied the peach-lit moon in the mauve December sky and thus recalled St. Thérèse's conversion as a teenager on a luminous Christmas Eve.

" Oh, dear!" I exclaimed aloud. "I almost forgot my Day Eight novena prayer!" So, while driving, I prayed the 24 Glory Be's in a humble petition for my saint's intercession.

"I needn't a sign that God will free me from my marriage to Carl, but I need the grace to bear the relationship until God wills my release," I prayed with each Glory Be.

No sooner had I completed the Glory Be's than my phone chimed. The caller was my sibling Miriam, a sister with the Congregation of Merciful Jesus (CMJ).

"Hey, Marise! I have something for you," she announced. "Drop by when you have a minute."

When I arrived at Miriam's apartment later that night, she handed me a small gift box.

"I saw Fr. Weston after Mass this morning at the CMJ Motherhouse, and he asked me to give this to you," she proclaimed, brimming with excitement.

I returned a puzzled gaze. Fr. Weston was the parish priest years ago at St. Augustine's, where he befriended my aging parents, who were longtime parishioners.

I last spoke with Fr. Weston four years ago when, upon my engagement to Carl, I contacted the priest about blessing our marriage. But per ecclesial protocol, he politely declined the honor.

With eager hands, I opened the box, and then ... I swooned. Before me lay a luminous rosary with beads of white, each splendid bead adorned with a delicate rosette of silver gilding. Astonished, I gazed at the rosary with untold wonder.

Derived from the Latin word "rosarium," rosary means rose garden, and a white rose is the signature sign that The Little Flower hears our prayer through the 24 Glory Be Novena.

Indeed, I petitioned the saint's intercession seeking only grace sufficient for my troubled marriage. Thus, she handpicked a garland of spiritual roses through a rosary gifted to me.

"He sent a card, too," Miriam pronounced, beaming. I opened the Christmas card and then read aloud the handwritten note inside:

"Marise, St. Peter Claver is entombed in the Church of St. Peter Claver
in Cartagena, Columbia. After praying there, I purchased this rosary."
Fr. Weston

"Fr. Weston recently visited the Shrine of St. Peter Claver in Cartagena, Columbia, where he purchased two rosaries – a brown one and a white one," Miriam explained. "He planned to give both rosaries to Fr. Pepe at Jesus Sun of Justice, but he opted to give the white one to you."

I sat astonished at the uncanny rosary resting in my palm.

Indeed, what was the chance that while praying a novena to The Little Flower for my troubled marriage, I would receive a white rosebud rosary from the shrine of the saint whose namesake was that of my wedding reception hall?

What was the chance I would receive the rosary from the priest I first contacted about blessing the marriage?!

But why would Fr. Weston give the rosary to me? I pondered.

Then, I recalled seeing the priest one month ago at the Consecration Mass of the new Jesus Sun of Justice Church.

Minutes before the bishop's grand procession into the sanctuary, I stationed myself near a back wall in the crowded gathering space inside the beautiful new church, where more than fifty diocesan priests formed a line awaiting entrance into the sanctuary.

Upon hearing the rustle of vestments, I glanced over my shoulder to spot Fr. Weston standing directly behind me.

"Hello, Fr. Weston; I'm so glad to see you here!" I whispered with ebullience.

He returned an ardent smile.

"If it weren't for you, Father, I wouldn't be here tonight," I remarked.

"Why is that?" he whispered.

I recounted that I contacted him four years before about blessing my marriage, at which he advised me to register in a parish and start attending Mass.

"I found Jesus Sun of Justice Church and started going to Mass, and now here I am!" I exclaimed.

"Did you marry the gentleman?" the priest queried.

"Um... yes," I replied with a bit of hesitation, "perhaps we can visit sometime?"

Fr. Weston nodded assent. But then the priests' line moved forward, moving him out of earshot, after which I never saw him again.

I could only conclude my chance meeting with Fr. Weston as the work of Providence. Within the church's large, crowded gathering area that night, I randomly chose to stand where Fr. Weston's spot in line halted, inviting our brief exchange.

Cradling the rosary in my hands, I shared with Miriam my novena petition and the circumstance leading to it.

Together, we marveled at the metaphysical phenomenon by which multiple, unrelated elements over four years—Fr. Weston, Jesus Sun of Justice Church, St. Peter Claver, marriage, novenas, and white roses—converged with impeccable timing that night into the embodiment of a white rosebud rosary.

Too exhilarated for sleep because of the supernatural gift, I sat awake in the soft moonlight before dawn, attempting to penetrate the divine message of the rosary from the Shrine of St. Peter Claver.

St. Peter Claver, a Spanish missionary and self-declared "slave of Negroes forever," dedicated his life to alleviating the suffering of enslaved Africans in the port city of Cartegena, Columbia, stated the leaflet that came with the rosary.

He ministered to the most abused and rejected of all people but spent the last four years of his life confined by illness and neglect. Yet he never complained.

I could only picture the humble priest on his sickbed, begging God for grace sufficient to bear his confinement: humility, patience, kindness, self-control, and understanding. Only through grace could the aging "slave of Negros forever" look beyond his own suffering to see with charity the suffering of his assigned caregiver, a former slave confined in spirit by the wounds of slavery.

The Spanish priest comforted those enslaved in the ships' holds and in the depths of their brokenness. The would-be saint expected nothing in return, nor did he expect from his caregiver what the former slave in wounded spirit could not give.

God does not expect me to heal the wounds Carl bears as a Black man in a country with deep roots of racism, my soul intuited. Nor does he ask me to heal the brokenness wrought by those wounds—the cultural, familial, and personal wounds that render vulnerability with self and others beyond his emotional reach.

Instead, God calls me to look beyond my own wounds to see with charity Carl's suffering. As St. Peter Claver expected nothing from those he served, God enjoins me to expect nothing from Carl that he cannot give for his woundedness.

I pondered Carl's cross in his vision loss and the uncanny onset of his vision impairment, which began the year our twins were born.

After our twins were born, we suspected vision problems in Gavin. So, Carl and I joined hands in prayer one day, whereby he prayed a selfless, impassioned entreaty for our son, "Dear God, please, please, please take my vision and let Gavin have his."

Indeed, months later, Carl's vision began to fade, and ten years later, complications from his glaucoma rendered him legally blind. But our son's vision was self-corrected and remains intact today.

I clasped the crucifix of the white rosebud rosary and thus meditated upon the Passion of Jesus and the helpers God stationed along the Way of the Cross.

Veronica wiped Jesus' scourged face, and Simon the Cyrenean eased the weight of the cross.

The weeping women bathed Jesus's agony with the balm of compassion. His mother, Mary, and apostle, John, stayed present to his suffering unto his hour of death upon the cross.

But alas! In the light of a luminous winter moon, my reflection revealed the mystical message embodied by the rosary.

My stalled relationship with Carl speaks not to the dismal imprisonment of a relationship dead but to the joyous invitation to grow in the virtue of charity.

God appointed each helper to comfort the suffering Jesus on his way to the cross. So, likewise, God appointed me to help Carl bear the cross of blindness with understanding, patience, kindness, and humility, if only until our children reach the age of eighteen.

More so, as St. Peter Claver, through confinement by illness, grew toward perfection in charity, so too might I, through confinement to a relationship, thus increase the virtue of charity.

I bowed my head and prayed the Day Nine novena prayer, offering praise and thanksgiving to God and St. Thérèse for the profound message of divine love embodied in the white rosebud rosary cradled in my palm.

God is good!

— ❧ —

To: Marise Gallica
From: Theodore Locherbie

Subject: Remarks—"The Rosary"

Marise,

This chapter held me spellbound from the first page! Upon reading your narrative a second time, I appreciated the interconnections from previous stories, with the spiritual connections especially impressive.

I was intrigued by the connection between the church's pianos at your home and the partial help and healing they provided you.

Despite playing the pianos to deflect the painful task of addressing your relationship issues and the source of your writer's block, your narrative speaks of the help and healing the pianos provided you.

But then you seized the opportunity of the Thanksgiving meal to reset your relationship with Marjorie, revealing God's intercession.

Namely, it seems too coincidental that you discovered through a phone conversation with another sister the day before Thanksgiving that Marjorie would spend Thanksgiving Day alone.

Yet, without these factors coming into play simultaneously, you wouldn't have had time alone with Marjorie for healing.

I stand in awe at the interconnectedness of your novena to the Little Flower and the white rosebud rosary gift from Fr. Weston as implicating a divine sign that your saint heard your prayer.

Moreover, I am dumbfounded by the connection you draw between St. Peter Claver in his ministry to enslaved Black persons and the various "crosses" of slavery, the burdens of oppression in modern times that Carl has faced.

This connection provided insight that you should grow in charity toward Carl, as did St. Peter Claver, who ascended in divine love toward his caregiver, a former slave, despite his caregiver's neglect.

Regards, Theodore Locherbie

To: Theodore Locherbie
From: Marise Gallica

Subject: Remarks - "The Rosary"

Mr. Locherbie,

Thank you for your remarks on my narrative, "The Rosary."

I heard you are retiring at the end of the school year. How wonderful for you! But how unfortunate for students who will not have the privilege of learning the art of writing from you, the legendary sage of Victory Prep Academy.

I realize that the spring semester is a busy time. So, I'm sending the final three chapters of my book to allow you time to review them before your last day in the classroom.

Thank you again for your time and effort in providing meaningful feedback on my book.

Regards, Marise

Chapter 12 Water into Wine

Dear St. Thérèse,

My story, "Water into Wine," reveals my discovery of an obscure truth in the Gospel story of the Wedding at Cana, a gem often overshadowed by the miracle of Jesus transforming water into wine in the famous wedding feast.

In friendship, Marise

Water into Wine

Christmastide

I marveled for days at my supernatural gift of the white rosebud rosary, which I had received only days before on a luminous December evening.

Indeed, with my newfound certainty of being seen, heard, affirmed, cherished, and blessed by God, the supernatural gift animated my soul with joy throughout Christmastide, the liturgical season beginning on Christmas Eve and concluding thirteen days later with the Feast of the Epiphany.

More so, the sacred meaning of the gift infused me with a yearning for spiritual nourishment beyond my daily prayer and weekly Mass attendance.

So, a week later, I sought spiritual sustenance at a New Year's Eve retreat at the Cana Retreat Center.

Billed as a retreat in observance of the Solemnity of Mary, Mother of God, whose Feast Day is January 1, the three-hour program promised a quiet evening of theological reflection on Mary.

I settled into a seat at a round table in the Center's conference hall that night, eager to gain new spiritual insight into the motherhood of Mary as well as my own motherhood.

Minutes later, the priest-facilitator for the retreat welcomed the group of fifty or so retreatants, offered an opening prayer, and then distributed handouts to each table.

"I invite everyone to silent reading and meditation over the Gospel passage on your handout," the priest announced, "after which I'll share a few theological reflections on Mary, and then you'll have the opportunity for small group discussion at each respective table."

Someone passed me a handout, and my eyes darted to the title, at which point my eager anticipation of the evening vanished.

The Gospel reading that night was "The Wedding at Cana" (John 2:1 -12). But my soaring Christmastide joy plummeted as images of the wedding feast narrative skittered through my imagination.

I sat crestfallen, dismayed that the retreat's theme that night was marriage instead of motherhood, as I'd hoped. Undoubtedly, the program's Gospel selection reflected the Church's obsession with the vocation of marriage, which renders invisible the spiritual needs and gifts of unmarried Catholics.

Indeed, upon arriving at the Center that night, I passed through the main entrance, where the sidewalk leads guests through a Wedding at Cana statuary.

The near-life-size bronze sculptures portray Mary enjoining Jesus to intervene in the situation of the depleted wine, the joyful wedding couple standing together, and nearby, the steward with a goblet in hand and the servants with water vessels.

Of course, I often mused that the statuary was befitting a space designed for engaged and married couple retreats. Nonetheless, whenever I passed by it, I winced at my lifelong feelings of emptiness in relationships.

More so, I avoided the Center on couples' retreat weekends. Seeing happy couples holding hands and gazing lovingly at each other overwhelmed me with the shame of my hollow marriage.

My eyes brimmed with tears at the shame of never having been authentically chosen for marriage. I sank my head to hide my untoward tears from the co-retreatants at my table and then calculated whether to stay or bolt.

Unable to decide, I elected to pray.

"The timeworn interpretation of the Wedding at Cana Gospel informs me that only married couples are worthy of the rich wine of His Presence in a relationship," I prayed.

"This Gospel pricks the painful belief of my unworthiness for a joyful marriage. Please, God, reveal a new meaning of this Gospel that is affirming for all persons, be they married or unwed."

With the hope that God heard my plea, I opted to stay, at least through the group discussion portion of the program. Thus, I meditated upon the Wedding of Cana narrative.

But my meditation yielded only a marriage-centric interpretation of the story, as did the priest's theological reflection a few minutes later. So, I begged the Holy Spirit to illuminate a new meaning of the story.

Lo! In that instant, the Holy Spirit elucidated a new truth of the narrative: The vessels represent our lives and souls, and the water represents our human interconnectedness.

So, first, Jesus tells us to fill our lives with relationships. Then, when we invite him into those relationships, he transforms our ordinary human connections into the rich wine of joyful, abundant human interconnection.

The truth of His transformative Presence is universal to all human connections, the Holy Spirit intimated to me. So, be the relationship ordinary or treasured, be it with a partner or friend, parent or child, sibling or family, coworker or teammate, neighbor, stranger, community, or nation; when we invite His presence, He transforms the relationship.

I sat astounded.

Over a lifetime of hearing only marriage-centric interpretations of the Gospel narrative, I recollected none that revealed the unspoken truth of His Presence in all relationships.

Three hours later, I joined my co-retreatants for New Year's Eve Mass in the Chapel of Mary the First Disciple, where I offered gratitude to the Holy Spirit for elucidating the life-giving truth of the Wedding at Cana story.

But the following day, an unexpected phone call revealed the priceless gem of truth hidden in the Wedding at Cana story.

New Year's Day

I attended New Year's Day Mass the next morning at Jesus Sun of Justice, during which Fr. Pepe's homily spoke of the grace of forgiveness.

I sat puzzled throughout the sermon, uncertain how the concept of forgiveness aligned with that day's Old Testament scripture about the light of God or the Gospel about shepherds laying eyes on the newborn Jesus.

Yet as Mass proceeded, I could only reflect on my need to forgive my sister, Marla. My favorite sister growing up, Marla, and I shared exuberant sibling camaraderie as young adults. Yet as middle-aged women, we hadn't spoken for a year.

Our falling out stemmed from a narrative I wrote about my childhood, which I shared with her a year ago.

My story, which referenced painful family history, met with harsh rebuke from Marla and another sister, Marjorie. For a year after the debacle, neither sister spoke to me nor did I to them.

Finally, after months of no contact, I summoned the courage to reach out to Marjorie with a homemade Thanksgiving feast. And lo, through the grace of kindness and hospitality, we reset our relationship that day by sharing the meal.

But my relationship with Marla remained broken, especially after my apology went unacknowledged. So, true to my fearful-avoidant attachment style of childhood, I disconnected from the relationship; the emptiness of disconnection registered less pain than the shame of rejection.

"So, eleven months hence, Marla and I still aren't speaking," I prayed after Holy Communion.

"My sister is angry, and I am wounded, God. The vessel of our relationship is broken; our interconnection has run dry. I beg you, Blessed Mary, please ask Jesus to heal our relationship."

Despite my prayer, I departed church feeling too vulnerable to reach out to Marla. Yet, upon arriving home, I spotted my white rosebud rosary on the table where I'd left it that morning.

But in that instant, a movement of the Spirit emboldened me to risk being vulnerable and call my sister Marla, hoping that sharing the remarkable story of the rosary gift might invite Jesus' healing presence into our relationship.

Without hesitation, I called Marla at once, and to my pleasant surprise, she answered with an ardent hello.

We chatted briefly about our jobs and children, and then in awkward silence, I whispered, "Marla, I have a marvelous story to share," to which she exclaimed, "I'd love to hear your story, Marise!"

With unrestrained exuberance, I shared my story of the white rosebud rosary.

"What an amazing story and gift," she remarked. "Can I see a picture of the rosary?"

I forwarded a photo of the rosary without further prompting, after which we opined about its beauty.

Then our phone call segued into warm humor and banter, shared interests and concerns, a joyful conversation reminiscent of the interconnection we shared years ago. Finally, an hour later, we bid fond goodbyes, pledging to stay in touch more often.

Afterward, I contemplated an alternative account of the Wedding at Cana story, where the steward, servants, hosts, and guests quarreled over the depleted wine.

Thus Mary, observing their interconnectedness run dry, enjoined her son, Jesus, to intervene.

So, as the discontented lot filled the vessels with water as Jesus instructed, kindness displaced petulance, joy overtook anger, forgiveness healed wounds and thereby did Jesus restore the abundant pleasure of everyone's human interconnection.

I cradled my white rosebud rosary in my palm, rejoicing at the restoration of my treasured interconnection with my sister and the truth of His Presence to heal relationships wounded and broken.

God is good!

Chapter 13 The Prayer Mantle

Dear St. Thérèse,

My story, "The Prayer Mantle," speaks of the oft' unheralded truth of Mary, the Blessed Mother, who hastens to protect us from the oppressors of our interior world to which we so often are blind.

In friendship, Marise

The Prayer Mantle

The Silence

The first six months of the COVID-19 pandemic found me increasingly exhausted. Nonetheless, I was determined to push through an unrelenting night shift schedule at Mercy Senior Care Hospital.

Yet, despite the pandemic demand for nurses, the company forced my resignation after I intervened on behalf of a Black coworker targeted with microaggressions.

While I've witnessed countless microaggressions toward Black persons, I had never dared interfere. But my intervention for my coworker marked my first time breaking the silence of complicity.

"I hope I didn't make you uncomfortable," I whispered to my coworker later that day. "And I hope my intervention won't cause retaliation."

"What you did was perfectly ok," she remarked. "I appreciate that you were there for me."

Yet, I never fathomed that my intervening might invite silent retaliation toward me—a white woman. But after departing Mercy Hospital, my rumination on the situation recalled a statement from.Fr. Zachary's first homily as a new pastor at Jesus Sun of Justice: "... prepare to be flogged from all sides" (Jeremiah 20: 10-13).

A chilling analogy of the mockery and torture, the "terror on all sides," which prophet Jeremiah withstood for being a spokesperson for God, the statement, as I understood it then, meant being prepared to risk rejection for witnessing to one's faith.

But upon my forced resignation from Mercy Hospital, I experienced the statement in a new light: risking rejection to protect the dignity of a marginalized person.

Indeed, the manager's refusal to acknowledge her microaggression felt like flogging by silence. Likewise, the CEO's complicity of silence to the microaggression also felt like flogging by silence.

To assert that my effort to preserve my coworker's dignity called forth flogging by silence from all sides would be a misstatement, for I shared the story with coworkers and others, who applauded my intervention.

Unfortunately, but ironically, sharing my story with others led to flogging by silence by yet another person—a priest, no less.

After sharing my story with others, I recognized that pride in the aftermath of my intervention tarnished my good deed. So, to confess my sin of pride, I sought the Sacrament of Reconciliation one Saturday afternoon at St. Augustine's, the parish of my childhood faith formation.

But my confession went nothing as I hoped and instead went something like this:

"Forgive me, father, for I have sinned," I began. "My last confession was about eight months ago. I'm here today because I intervened on behalf of a Black coworker whom the manager targeted with verbal microaggressions. But my pride sullied what otherwise might've been a quiet but shining moment of standing against oppression. For that, I am sorry."

"Pardon me, when was your last confession?" queried the priest's voice behind the screen.

"Um… about eight months ago," I stammered, taken aback by the query.

"Is that the only sin you've committed in eight months?" questioned the monotone voice.

"No, Father," I replied with exasperation, "I'm sure I have more sins I can't recall."

Vexed that the priest deemed my long-forgotten venial sins more sinful than the sin that brought me to confession that day, I sat speechlessly, unable to articulate further my undue pride.

Yet, without a word of theological reflection, wisdom, or insight, the priest abruptly assigned me a penance of three Hail Marys.

I then prayed aloud an Act of Contrition and whispered, "Amen," after which the priest delivered the absolution in a curt, robotic tone.

I departed the confessional in a silent huff. I've had a warmer dialog with the drive-thru attendant at the burger shack, I grumbled. But more so, I was hurt.

I anticipated neither a medal of courage for my excellent deed nor extended time in the confessional to discuss my undue pride in its aftermath.

But I hoped the priest might offer theological reflection on the immanence of God's grace to guide me toward holiness. Yet none were forthcoming.

That night, I contemplated the Gospel of the woman about to be stoned for adultery. I couldn't imagine that Jesus would halt in the street before pardoning the woman, only to question when was her last atonement at the temple and was adultery her *only* transgression?

Moreover, I couldn't fathom Jesus to have uttered token words of absolution, absent words of mercy.

My transgression and distress were neither the glaring sin of adultery nor a chanting mob poised to stone me for it.

Instead, my transgression was the deadly sin of pride, and my distress was the hissing asp in my mind hellbent on shaming me for it—or so I thought.

"I felt unseen and unheard at confession today," I prayed. "The priest neither acknowledged my sin nor the circumstance leading to it. So, I departed feeling not reconciled with God but flogged by silence by the priest's dismissive attitude."

Hence, I prayed that God grant me peace from the silent flogging doled out by the CEO, the manager, and now, of all persons, a priest!

The next six weeks found me scrambling for a paycheck, but more so, waiting for God to grant me peace over my departure from Mercy Senior Care Hospital.

Finally, on a Friday weeks later, I received a call from a nursing staffing agency offering an immediate contract as a COVID-19 nurse at La Pradera Community Hospital, forty miles south of my home.

So, three days later, I donned my scrubs and stethoscope and began my first shift on the COVID unit in the twelve-bed hospital, where I would provide night-shift nursing for the next six months.

I wouldn't have accepted a COVID nursing position were it not for me and my sons the day before completing a ten-day quarantine for testing positive for the virus.

Fortunately, we experienced only mild symptoms. So, having already had the virus in my household, I had no fear of caring for COVID patients.

The Prayer Mantle

Nonetheless, two months after leaving Mercy Senior Care Hospital, the First Sunday of Advent found me indignant over my forced resignation.

Yet, while meditating after Holy Communion that day, I finally realized that my resistance to forgiveness, not my sin of pride, was the root of my resentment.

Thus, at that moment, I forgave the manager who perpetrated the microaggression, the CEO who forced my resignation, and the priest whose manner made me feel unseen and unheard.

Then, I begged Mary, the Mother of Jesus, to please ask God to heal me so I could heal others.

That night, I worked with Elena, a longtime registered nurse at the hospital who belonged to Our Lady of Guadalupe Church in the tight-knit community of La Pradera. And in the pre-dawn hush at the nurses' station, we shared stories of our faith. But I never disclosed to Elena, nor anyone, the circumstance of my departure from Mercy Senior Care Hospital.

Four nights later, we worked together again. "I have something for you," Elena announced, handing me a cheerful, red floral prayer mantle tied with blue yarn.

My coworker's gift rendered me speechless.

Upon asking Blessed Mother for healing, I anticipated neither a visible sign that she heard my prayer nor a gift from anyone.

Yet, only days later, I held the unexpected gift of a prayer mantle from a new coworker stitched by none other than the ladies of the Prayer Mantle Ministry of Our Lady of Guadalupe Church!

I knew that Our Lady of Guadalupe is the patroness of Latin America and that the Church sees her as a symbol of justice because she holds an appeal to the poor and marginalized people. Thus, the Catholic faithful can see her as representing persons who stand against oppression.

Indeed, the card attached to the prayer mantle read:

"This prayer mantle has been prayed over and blessed at Our Lady of Guadalupe's Healing Mass. Be healed in Jesus' name, we pray."

Lo! When I stood helpless against the oppressors of my interior world—anger, pride, spite, and disordered attachment to my wound—I prayed to Mary, and she heard my plea. Through the gift of a prayer mantle, blessed by the church of her namesake, Our Lady covered me with prayer, and thus she healed me that night.

God is good!

Chapter 14 The Landscape

Dear St. Thérèse,

My narrative, "The Landscape," portrays how the movement of the Holy Spirit led me to find healing decades after the sudden death of a friend.

The import of this story lies not in the circumstance of his death but in the invitation for transformation delivered to me decades later.

In friendship, Marise

The Landscape

The Wall

A year after Carl and I were married, a Friday in mid-June found us driving on the interstate to pick up our thirteen-year-old son, Devin, from music camp. Yet, typical for the year since we wed, the tension between us was taut with stonewalling.

As we approached the city of Valley Hope, a roadside sign for The Newland Institute caught my eye.

"The Newland Institute is off that exit," I pronounced, breaking the awkward silence.

"I covered it when I was a staff writer at the *Valley Hope Herald* in my previous career," I explained, to which Carl offered no response.

Nonplussed at no bite for the bait of a casual conversation, I fell silent, during which I recalled Tevis, an intern at The Newland Institute who was my source for stories twenty-seven years ago.

In the decades since, I traveled the interstate corridor countless times, and I usually thought of Tevis whenever I passed the sign.

But no matter where I was, I always thought of Tevis in late June.

"A Newland Institute intern disappeared one summer, and two weeks later, his body was found in a wheat field," I declared.

"What happened?" Carl queried, gazing at the smartphone tethered to his earphones.

"He overdosed," I replied, silently noting that I had never mentioned Tevis nor my coverage of Newland Institute to Carl in twenty-seven years.

In fact, I mused in silence; I never told anyone my Newland source once asked me out.

"A farmer spotted a body in the field from the cab of the combine," I recounted to Carl,

"The intern's ten-speed bike with sneakers, a note, and an empty pill bottle was found nearby. Tevis was my contact at Newland; he was the only person I had personally known to take his life."

"That's nothing, Marise," Carl muttered with an unbroken stare at his smartphone screen. "I've known so many people who've taken their lives. And you've only known one?"

"Why do you always ruin our time, bringing up negative memories!" he exclaimed. "Can't you be positive for once?"

I might've offered words of solace to Carl at having lost so many friends to suicide. But his contempt, criticism, and defensiveness shut me out and shut me down.

So, in despair, I sealed another stone into the impenetrable wall between us.

But Tevis' memory stayed with me, and I pondered the prospect of reaching out to his parents. I considered doing so after the ordeal ended so many years ago.

But what was the purpose, I recalled asking myself. At a loss for words in the weeks following Tevis' death, I decided to move forward and not look back.

Nonetheless, I considered connecting with Tevis' parents for decades each year in June. But each year, the notion felt incrementally more awkward and inappropriate, intrusive and inauthentic, and needy and self-serving.

Who was I but a stranger to contact the couple unexpectedly about their long-deceased son? I could only imagine my contact reseeding the family's grief anew and shuttering any hope for an authentic connection. Hence, I never acted on the notion.

That Sunday, Father's Day, I attended 11 a.m. Mass at Jesus Sun of Justice. Upon returning to my pew after Communion, I recalled that it was Father's Day when Tevis' father, Franklin Brock, learned of his son's disappearance the previous day in June 1990.

A 1989 graduate of Bluestem College, Tevis was a standout math and physics scholar at the school, where he earned enviable honors in an international mathematics competition.

The summer of 1990 found him working the research plots as an intern at The Newland Institute, an alternative agriculture research organization in rural Valley Hope.

Franklin, an agronomy professor at State College, and his wife Sheryl would spend the next two weeks in Valley Hope that summer desperately searching, hoping, and praying for the safe return of their twenty-three-year-old son. Although I interviewed Tevis' father, Franklin, over the phone while covering the story, I never met the couple.

"Something moves me, again, to reach out to Tevis' parents, but I fear risking vulnerability and shame for insensitivity to the family's loss," I confided to God after Communion.

Then, a voice of unidentified origin whispered to my soul, "Marise, risking vulnerability might yield the authentic connection you seek."

I departed Mass that day determined to contact Tevis' parents.

Unsure of words to connect with them, I prayed for a meaningful connection. But, more profoundly, I begged God for the grace of compassion to accept the couple's response, be it favorable or unfavorable or the forever uncertainty of no response.

But lost that day was attunement to the Holy Spirit as the voice encouraging me to contact Tevis' parents. More so, I was unaware of the spiritual journey that would launch the following day, a journey that, unbeknownst to me, lay idle since 2015.

The Garden

The next morning, a magnificent sunrise heralded the start of a new day. Moved to optimism by a spacious sky infinite with hope, I elected to compose a brief note of belated condolence for the couple, which I would send to Franklin Brock's faculty email at State College.

Intending to craft no more than a thoughtful, one-paragraph message to the couple, I thus began to write. But then, thirty minutes later, upon the screen before me lay a 1,200-word narrative that, for twenty-seven years, percolated through the bedrock of my subconscious.

Herewith follows that narrative, cast as an email message, and the couple's response.

From: Marise Gallica

To: Franklin and Sheryl Brock

Hello Franklin and Sheryl,

My name is Marise Gallica. You don't know me, but I keep you in my thoughts every year as the warm, windy days of June melt into ethereal sunsets over the wheat fields of Kansas. I was a reporter for the *Valley Hope Herald* in the summer of 1990.

I want to express how deeply sorry I am for the loss of your dear son, Tevis. I've spent years in angst as to whether to contact you. Grief has an uncanny way of reseeding itself over time, and I wanted to be sensitive to your grief journey.

After decades of prayer and reflection, though, I am compelled to reach out to you, as I hope that sharing how I knew Tevis offers a bit of continued healing for each of us in our own way.

I met Tevis in April 1990 while I was a staff writer for the *Valley Hope Herald*, covering The Newland Institute. The Institute was part of my environmental, science, and health beat.

I was writing a feature on Newland, where Tevis would show me the garden. Wearing khaki cargo shorts and a green t-shirt, he enthusiastically showed me the garden crops.

He was especially pleased with the progress of the strawberries, row upon row of sturdy, leafy green plants bejeweled with scores of plump red berries.

After a tour of the garden, which yielded three pages of notes, I headed back to the *Herald* office to draft my story. Under the guise of "wanting to get the story right," I called him over the next few days. But I found him a fascinating conversationalist with an effusive passion for the environment.

I worked with Tevis on more stories for Newland. Then, one day while chatting over the phone about yet another news article, Tevis asked me for dinner. I wasn't expecting a dinner invitation, but I was thrilled.

I really wanted to meet him for dinner!

He was so kind and easy to talk to. I saw in him a gentle spirit and a lovable and compassionate human being whom I wanted to get to know better.

But I declined. With an apology, I told Tevis that journalists aren't supposed to fraternize with their sources because doing so could pose a conflict of interest. He shrugged it off, and we continued the interview.

My reason for declining was only partially valid.

Truth be known, I was a twenty-four-year-old, unwed mother with a toddler from what at the time was a long-distance relationship, which went defunct three years later.

I wasn't ready to risk a more meaningful relationship. And, of course, I didn't quite know Tevis well enough to ascertain whether he was asking me out because he liked me or if he was asking me to dinner as "just a friend."

Tevis disappeared two days later. Along with other *Herald* news staff, I covered the ensuing search during the long, anxious days from when Tevis disappeared until a farmer found his body two weeks later.

The morning Tevis' body was found, I was asleep and dreaming. In my dream, which I recall vividly, I was in the Mathematics Hall at Bluestem College.

I was standing in the foyer. Late afternoon sunbeams were streaming through the main doors, where the main lecture hall was dark and vacant.

The foyer door clicked, and then Tevis burst through the door. He wore a bright red t-shirt, khaki cargo shorts, well-worn running-turned-gardening shoes, and his round, wire-rimmed glasses. Tevis was grinning ear-to-ear.

"Marise!" he called, his prominent Adam's apple resonating with his soft, bass-toned voice.

I smiled. "So this is where you went to school!" I exclaimed.

"Yes! This is Bluestem College!" Tevis remarked, beaming.

We approached each other with arms outstretched as if to embrace in a warm, peaceful, all-is-well hug.

Then, the phone rang. It was 8:30 a.m. Saturday, June. 30, 1990. The caller was Joan, the *Herald's* weekend news desk editor.

In a subdued tone, Joan informed me that the police found Tevis' body. The news desk thought I might want to know before the local media broadcast because I had been covering the story.

I sat up, stunned. Shock. Sadness. Compassion. Guilt. Loss. The feelings washed over me for weeks.

I've tried to find meaning in my dream about Tevis for years. So the timing of the phone call was, indeed, uncanny.

The abstract dimensions of time and space, existence and being, have fascinated philosophers and mathematicians since the beginning of humankind.

Likewise, humans desperately want to believe that our souls can traverse the dimensions of time and space, even if we can't understand them.

Being the math whiz he was, Tevis' soul was in its element, hopping and skipping through the quantum physics of time and space. I could only wonder if that was his first foray into the time and space dimension, and he was grinning at how amazing it was.

My heart tells me Tevis wanted me to know he "made it" all right and that he is happy and all will be well. But unfortunately, my rational brain tells me that's not what death means.

Through the years, I've wondered, had I gone to dinner with Tevis, would his life, and mine, have taken a different turn?

Did he take his life because I didn't go out with him? But, on the other hand, could I have helped him and been a much-needed friend when he felt hopeless?

Please know I would have done whatever I could to help Tevis. I am so sorry that Tevis is gone. His was a beautiful and gentle spirit that I feel walks with me sometimes, even today, especially when I look out over the vast prairie of Kansas.

The attached picture is of me three summers ago at El Camino Heights, south of Valley Hope. I feel Tevis' connection to nature and his beautiful spirit in places like this.

Sincerely, Marise

I clicked Send and then sought the distraction of work to avert obsessing over my message.

-------- ⤫ --------

Later that afternoon, though, Franklin replied. With trembling uncertainty, I perused his email:

From: Franklin Brock

To: Marise Gallica

Subject: Thinking of you

Dear Marise,

Thank you, Marise, for reaching out to us with your heartfelt condolences and the highly personal story of your interviews with Tevis twenty-seven years ago.

We were both very touched by your feelings, dream, and courage to write and share your experiences with Tevis at The Newland Institute. Your thoughtful description of your encounters with Tevis confirmed to us the kind of person he was.

Your letter took us back to the prairie, our experiences after Tevis' disappearance, and the devastating news of his death. Of course, we think of him often and wonder how things might have turned out differently. We hope that your sharing brings you comfort and even closure.

Sheryl will also send a short message now, and we will write to you as we digest your experiences and reflect on them.

Thank you for writing, and you will hear from us.

With love, Franklin and Sheryl

I exhaled a deep sigh of relief. Indeed, Sheryl responded a brief time later.

-------- ⤫ --------

To: Marise Gallica

From: Sheryl Brock

Subject: Keeping in touch

Dear Marise,

Tears are streaming down my face! We are beyond words with gratitude that you reached out to us, Marise.

We are at the Bluestem Municipal Airport awaiting departure to visit Tevis' younger brother, Kyle. We are gazing at a beautiful summer sky, filled with hope at what you have described in your letter. We will be in touch with you.

Love and hugs, Sheryl

I wouldn't hear from the couple until the end of summer, and the intervening months found me despairing for a meaningful connection.

Finally, Sunday night of Labor Day weekend found me searching my email for my original message to Franklin and Sheryl. For closure, I needed to revisit my narrative as rendered into words on paper versus imagery in my mind.

Nonetheless, to my dismay, I realized that I accidentally and permanently deleted my message weeks earlier.

"You no doubt upset them with your letter," the verminous voices in my head rasped. "Tevis' parents don't know you and do not want to connect with you!"

My voice of reason joined the fray:

"Obsessing over your letter isn't healthy, Marise," urged my voice of reason. "So give it up!"

So, resigned to my despair, I released my yearning for connection with Tevis' parents and finally willed myself to sleep.

Later that day, I glanced at my email Inbox and discovered an unanticipated message from Sheryl with a timestamp of 5:28 a.m.

I sat astounded. Mere hours after I relinquished my need for connection, the connection I sought was delivered, embodied by Sheryl's email message:

To: Marise Gallica

From: Sheryl Brock

Subject: Keeping in touch

Hi Marise,

I think about your letter and see your photo more often than I write. We shared your letter with our son Kyle and daughter Kindra. Kindra remarked how courageous you were to write.

Your letter touched Kyle deeply. Tevis was his older brother, and they were close. But Kyle had no idea that Tevis would take his own life.

Reading your letter helped Kyle share his long-held feelings about losing Tevis, more so than he has in a long time. And that was important for all of us. So, we thank you for that.

We do hope to hear from you, Marise.

Much love and warm hugs to you, Sheryl

I could do nothing but absorb the warmth and affirmation of Sheryl's response. I replied to Sheryl later that evening.

To: Sheryl Brock

From: Marise Gallica

Subject: Keeping in touch

Hi Sheryl,

What a surprise to hear from you today!

I must say that "uncanny" must be the leitmotif of our communication. Last night I was searching for my original message to you and Franklin. But then I realized I accidentally deleted it recently while attempting long overdue inbox management.

I was concerned that my letter opened a painful wound for your family. So, with all due respect, I concluded that I would never hear from the Brock family again.

Nonetheless, I wanted to read our email thread. I use writing to process intense emotions, and the thoughts and feelings that manifested in my narrative email percolated in my subconscious for the better of twenty-seven years.

I read my email to you and Franklin countless times in the weeks after writing it.

Nonetheless, hours before receiving your email above, I determined I needed to let go of the Tevis Brock saga.

I figured my letter wreaked emotional havoc on your family. More so, obsessing about my letter can't be healthy. So, imagine my surprise at hearing from you this morning!

I am grateful that your son Kyle and daughter Kindra responded positively to my narrative about Tevis. I am from a large family; I can't fathom the pain, grief, anger, and loss I would experience at losing one of my siblings.

For Kyle, the void of Tevis' absence must be palpable. So, it is heartening to know that my letter opened the door for much-needed sharing.

Likewise, I am moved that Kindra recognized that my reaching out took courage. Of course, it's not easy to approach someone about the profoundly painful loss of one's child. But reaching out means taking a risk that might hurt either party or yield a meaningful connection.

I prayed for a meaningful connection. But I also prayed for the grace to accept with compassion whichever response my letter yielded.

Regards, Marise

To: Marise Gallica
    From: Sheryl Brock
    Subject: Keeping in touch
    Hi Marise,

Things happen for reasons we can't explain but are grateful for. Tevis is with us daily, so nothing you wrote opened wounds or wreaked emotional havoc on us.

It made me recall missed opportunities back then, which others have shared with us. But what's done, we cannot change. We are grateful that our lives are blessed with friends and opportunities for new experiences.

The recounting of your dream is beautiful and touching; we are grateful that you reached out to us with your letter. Be assured it was a meaningful connection.

Tell us about yourself if you'd like to. And please keep in touch. But if I don't answer in a timely manner, give me a little nudge. Things get lost in the stack sometimes.

Many hugs, Sheryl

Three years hence, we've yet to meet, Tevis' mother and me. But we're pen-pals, nonetheless.

Sheryl and Franklin, a retired emeritus professor, travel internationally for teaching and learning focused on agronomy, culture, and environmental justice. The connection, indeed, is authentic. Upon receiving every letter from Sheryl, I offer gratitude to God for the work of the Holy Spirit, which first moved me to reach out to Franklin and Sheryl.

The Vista

My connection with Sheryl lies not in our friendship but in the risk of making the connection. To take the chance was to answer a summons to transform into the authentic self that God created me to be.

Upon my first visit to Jesus Sun of Justice Church, I asked God to transform me. So, in Divine fashion, the universe responded, putting me at the scene of a highway accident two days later, whereby I experienced what I believe was the undeniable presence of God.

But I could not comprehend what the experience meant or what I was supposed to do with it. So, I did nothing.

Then, on Father's Day two years later, the Holy Spirit again enjoined me to act – this time to risk authentic connection. Yet to do so was far more terrifying than staying present to a helpless survivor of an accident on a dark, dangerous highway.

Resident in my subconscious and on constant alert crouched my deep-seated, life-long fear of seeking authentic connection – a fear rooted in my dismal history of meaningful relationships growing up and throughout adulthood.

Nonetheless, I summoned the courage to be vulnerable and reach out to Tevis' parents. And upon doing so, it was as if I crossed a supernatural threshold into an unknown, sacred space, after which my false identity of shame began to fracture.

A week after I contacted Tevis' parents, I accepted a new job, a soul-crushing stint of eight months that moved me to re-examine the true calling of my nursing vocation.

Later that year, upon receiving Holy Communion during a quiet weeknight Mass, my interior life fell into a veritable crucible of angst, marking the start of my adult life's most tumultuous but transformative interior period.

The subsequent epiphanies, synchronicities, insights, and movements of the Spirit feel no less than supernatural.

But the heart of my transformation was my evolving awareness that my disordered belief of unworthiness was based on unhealthy relationship patterns that I learned growing up.

Yet, until journaling "The Landscape," I'd forgotten about the photo I sent with my first email to Franklin and Sheryl.

My sons snapped my picture at the historic Camarillo Heights Park south of Valley Hope, where we'd ventured on a golden summer evening years ago.

Yet, upon revisiting the photo, my eyes were drawn not to my T-shirt-clad self in the foreground but to the breathtaking prairie vista usurping the background. Thus emerged the significance of my connection with Tevis' parents.

As a landscape artist enlivens the canvas with movement rendered as rippling water, fluttering butterflies, and sky-bound birds, so too, God breathes life into his masterpiece landscape of our lives.

Alas! God saw a subtle emptiness on my canvas, yearning to be enlivened with meaningful connection. Hence, through Franklin and Sheryl's warm affirmation, God thus breathed life and movement into that unfilled space that only He, the Divine artist, could see.

God is good!

Chapter 15 Jesus, Author of Life

To: Marise Gallica

    From: Theodore Locherbie

    Subject: Summary Remarks

    Marise,

    I've provided insights on how you could expand your ending to include all the meaningful experiences you've written about, but excellent development of all your stories!

    Through your personal encounters, painful struggles, and spiritual insights, you've scripted a meaningful novella that flows well, describes beautifully, expresses perceptibly, and engages readers!

    Your narratives are especially effective in providing insights about personal struggles that so many others experience and giving countless spiritual experiences revealing God's supernatural interventions in our lives, revealing that God is good.

    You are ready to publish this once you make minor corrections. Yet, what a gift of expression through writing you have.

    Thank you for inviting me into your writing and personal journeys that have grown you into the person you have become.

    Blessings! Theodore Locherbie

To: Theodore Locherbie

    From: Marise Gallica

Mr. Locherbie,

Congratulations on your retirement next Friday after fifty years of teaching! I planned to post my well-wishes to Victory Prep's social media post announcing your special day. But I keep revising my message to ensure its highest literary quality—a practice I learned from you.

You have been an enthusiastic teacher to the thousands of students who experienced (and survived!) Honors English under the tutelage of the legendary Mr. Locherbie. Words cannot express my gratitude for the gift of your writing mentorship, which you have shared so generously with me.

I believe the purpose of every human being's journey through life is to discover who God created them to be. So, along the way, God gifts each of us with "sages" or "teachers," whose guidance helps reveal our authentic selves.

Indeed, Mr. Locherbie, I believe that your name, "Theodore," which means "gift of God," reflects your gift for teaching the art of writing. But more so, your name reflects the gift of Divine Providence, which placed you, the legendary sage of Victory Prep Academy, along my journey so long ago and decades later to help me discover who God created me to be.

Blessings! Marise

Dear St. Thérèse,

I share with you the conclusion of this leg of my journey in the experience of being human. With deep gratitude, I thank you, St. Thérèse, for the gift of your spiritual companionship in my journey to discovering who God created me to be.

In friendship, Marise

Jesus, Author of Life

I attended the 11 a.m. Mass at Jesus Sun of Justice on Sunday, October 1, the Feast Day of St. Thérèse of Lisieux—a day designated by the Roman Catholic Church to celebrate the life of The Little Flower.

That Sunday also marked a special event for Jesus Sun of Justice Church, celebrating the blessing of its new prayer garden. Finished only days before, the installation of the prayer garden signified the completion of the church's four-year construction project.

The prayer garden featured more than six hundred commemorative pavers. Parishioners and friends of Jesus Sun of Justice Church donated the engraved bricks in honor of a living or deceased loved one or a sacred figure who has influenced their faith journey.

So, after Mass, one hundred parishioners gathered in the courtyard garden under a brilliant blue October sky to see the garden blessed, where, with prayers of praise and thanksgiving and a holy water sprinkler, Fr. Pepe blessed the sacred space.

After the blessing, the crowd dispersed to tour the garden—an area graced with the noble simplicity of a Holy Family statue set on a pedestal and the natural beauty of vibrant shrubs and flowering borders, made unique to the church for its commemorative paver bricks.

Indeed, dozens in the crowd gravitated to the paver brick area to search for their commemorative pavers, which formed the ground cover near the life-size statue of Mary, Joseph, and the child Jesus.

I lingered near the garden entrance, greeting parish friends and families until the group cleared, and then I meandered to the statue to search for my bricks.

But first, I paused to study the statue's details. Then, I was so engrossed that I didn't notice when Fr. Pepe drew beside me until he lightly tapped my arm.

"What a beautiful statue of The Holy Family and inspirational image for our church and school community," I whispered with warm surprise.

Fr. Pepe peered up at the statue and then back at me, "Yes, we are pleased with the garden," he remarked, beaming. "I believe the statue, paver bricks, and flowers and trees will make this a special place of prayer and reflection."

"I'm grateful for the commemorative bricks," I exclaimed. "I donated two bricks, and I'm eager to see them. But it might take me a while to find both among the hundreds here."

The kindly priest nodded assent and then bid me a good day, after which I glanced down at the pavers to search for my bricks. Then, I gasped!

Beneath the tip of my shoes where I stood, I spied my bricks inlaid next to each other—one proclaiming "Jesus, Author of Life" and one engraved with "El Roi." (In ancient scripture, "El Roi" means "the God Who Sees.")

I stood astonished at the sweet synchronicity, for what was the chance that out of six hundred bricks, I would stop and stand, unaware, upon my own two bricks?

Then, in that instant, I recalled that autumn Sunday four years ago at the old Jesus Sun of Justice Church when I attended my first Mass in years and begged God to transform me. So, in Divine fashion, the God Who Sees answered my plea.

He placed me at the scene of an accident on a dark, dangerous highway, unfolding a spiritual journey abundant with blessings unforeseen: vulnerability and courage, forgiveness and reconciliation, hope and healing, connection and relationship, epiphany and revelation.

I marveled at the petals of Divine Providence that marked every turn of my story—a story that only Jesus, Author of Life, could script.

Indeed, my spiritual journey has revealed the authentic self that God created me to be: a storyteller with the gift of narrating the human experience through the creative expression of writing.

Alas! Through the gift of spiritual companionship with St. Thérèse, I will be who God created me to be!

God is good!

About the Author

Peggy Phillips debuts her first work of fiction with the powerful and poignant epistolary novella "Letters to the Little Flower - The Gift of Spiritual Companionship with St. Therese of Lisieux." Born in Wichita, KS, Peggy grew up in a large Catholic family in a small Kansas town. Outside of her writing vocation, Peggy enjoys hiking the beautiful nature trails of Kansas and spending time with her family.

About the Publisher

Pradera Rosa Publishing House is devoted to publishing adult fiction in the spiritual and metaphysical genre.

www.ingramcontent.com/pod-product-compliance
Lightning Source LLC
Chambersburg PA
CBHW021445150726
47989CB00001B/406